When her gaze me... felt the spark, too. ... lightning whenever they were within arm's reach of each other.

Dr. Elwood Jackson. Still fine as ever.

A sexy smirk flashed across his face before it was replaced with…apathy. "Avery," he greeted.

"El," she replied, willing the warmth that had pooled in her belly away. "What are you doing here?" Avery gestured to the guard and waved him away. The burly six-foot-two man stepped back, giving her and El some space.

"Honestly, I don't know. Maybe I just wanted to come and see for myself if you were real. Or if you were a figment of my imagination."

The barb hurt, but she didn't blame him. The last time they'd seen each other hadn't been pleasant. Massaging her aching temple, she answered, "Touché."

They stood in silence, each of them taking the other in. His gaze traveled down the length of her body, causing the hairs on her arms to stand on end and her stomach to do the crazy flips it always did when he was near. Like a magnet, he made her want to step forward, right into his arms.

Dear Reader,

Some couples don't get it right the first time. *Wherever You Are* explores how a second chance at love can be so much sweeter.

A wise person once told me that "God will find a way to sit you down, to make you rest." Avery is at that point in her life, forced to rest due to a health crisis, and it's not easy for her. Dr. Elwood Jackson (El) is the man who helps Avery heal. He's also her first love. Their relationship didn't end well, but when she needs him—despite the hurt and betrayal of the past—he is there for her.

Wherever You Are deals with forgiveness and understanding, moving forward while dealing with the past. Most of all, it's about loving another person unconditionally, being willing to see the best in someone and loving them through the pain.

I hope you enjoy the ride!

Love,

Elle

ElleWright.com

@LWrightAuthor

WHEREVER *You* ARE

Elle Wright

HARLEQUIN® KIMANI™ ROMANCE

Recycling programs
for this product may
not exist in your area.

ISBN-13: 978-1-335-21673-1

Wherever You Are

Copyright © 2018 by Leslie Wright

Printed in U.S.A.

There was never a time when **Elle Wright** wasn't about to start a book, already deep in a book or just finishing one. She grew up believing in the importance of reading, and became a lover of all things romance when her mother gave her her first romance novel. She lives in Southeast Michigan.

Books by Elle Wright

Harlequin Kimani Romance

It's Always Been You
Wherever You Are

To my mother, Regina; you are missed.

Acknowledgments

I thank my God for His protection, His provision, His love. I would be nothing without Him.

To Jason; my children, Asante, Kaia, Masai; and the rest of my family, I love you all BIG. There are so many of you, I can't name everyone. But you know who you are. I learned long ago that you don't have to be blood to be family, and that couldn't be more true. I appreciate the time, the talks, the hugs, the tears…everything. I thank you all for your unwavering support.

To my agent, Sara, I thank you for believing in me.

To the Kimani family, thank you for your encouragement.

Hard to believe I'm on this journey. I couldn't have done it without all of your love and support. Thank you for being #TeamElle! You all mean the world to me!

Chapter 1

"Life is full of twists and turns, dips and hills."
Avery Montgomery viewed her audience. Some were
smiling; some were crying; some were simply listening. She'd rocked it! Every anecdote, every joke,
every story...on point. Who knew she could add public speaking to her already amazing résumé? But...
Ooo wee, is this what a hot flash feels like?

Avery pulled at her sweater and took a quick sip
of her water. As she viewed some of the hopeful
faces in the front row, she thought back on her college graduation many years ago and the view of life
she'd had back then. Graduating at the top of her
class in molecular biology was no small feat, and
she'd dreamed of being invited back one day to encourage young women of color to pursue careers in
math and science.

When she was twenty-one—the same age of many of those in front of her—she would have placed a wager that she'd be completing her residency right now and getting ready for a coveted fellowship at Johns Hopkins.

Yet she wasn't standing before the beautiful, intelligent graduates of the University of Michigan as Dr. Avery Montgomery. Instead, she was standing before them as Avery Montgomery, creator, head writer and executive producer of a top television show.

Giving the keynote address at the Black Celebratory, a program put in place to acknowledge and celebrate the African American experience at her alma mater, meant everything to her. Avery couldn't help but snicker at the irony, though. No Johns Hopkins. No residency. But she'd still been invited to inspire a room full of hopeful college graduates.

"Never be afraid to step outside of your comfort zone. Don't be afraid to fail. Embrace rejection, not because it's a part of life, but because it's a learning tool that will propel you to new heights," she continued, squeezing the podium.

Avery's gaze dropped down to her notes. The words blurred in front of her. Her head hurt in a way it had never hurt before. In fact, it was the worst headache of her life. But she pushed herself to keep going, as she did every day. *Okay, I got this.*

"You already know the standard platitudes given to graduates. Never let your major, your advisors, your parents or your friends prevent you from following your dream. That's very true. When I started my time here at the University of Michigan, I wasn't going to let anyone tell me I couldn't be a scientist, that I wouldn't become a doctor."

Glancing up from the podium, she met one of her favorite professors' eyes and smiled. Then she scanned the audience once again. "I stand before you…"

The word "today" died on her lips when she spotted the familiar silhouette in front of her, at the entrance of the auditorium. The massive Power Center was packed full of proud parents, giddy grandparents, solemn professors and others there to wish the 2018 graduating class much success. The spotlight was on her, but it might as well have been on him. She couldn't see his face, but there was no mistaking the man who had made her life on campus what she'd deem the best time of her life.

A flash from a camera jerked her thoughts back to the matter at hand. "I…" She covered by clearing her throat and taking another long gulp of water. "Today, I stand before you as someone who thought I knew my destiny—until I didn't. And that's okay." Unable to help herself, she looked at the entrance of the massive space again. He was gone.

"It's okay to veer off your predetermined road because your future may be off the map altogether. Be open to the possibilities of life," she said, in closing. "You won't regret it. Thank you."

Avery waved, took a quick bow and hugged Professor Bauer before an escort led her off the stage. When she'd accepted the formal invitation to speak, she'd hoped to stay behind and greet some of the students, but a last-minute change to her schedule prevented that.

She wasted no time unhooking the microphone from the lapel of her suit. Thanking her escort, she proceeded toward the waiting limousine with her security following close behind. Avery could hear the cheers from the auditorium as she walked, and she felt a pang of guilt for leaving before she could shake the hands of the graduates.

"Duty calls," she mumbled to herself with a quick roll of her eyes.

"No time to greet your fans?"

Avery tripped and almost hit the floor. Fortunately for her, that smooth baritone voice belonged to someone whose reflexes were unrivaled. His smell wrapped around her brain while his strong arms snaked around her waist, preventing her fall.

She backed out of his warm grasp quickly and tugged on her suit jacket. When her gaze met his, she knew he'd felt the spark, too. It was like a bolt of lightning whenever they were within arm's distance of each other.

Dr. Elwood Jackson. *Still fine as ever.*

A sexy smirk flashed across his face before it was replaced with...apathy. "Avery," he greeted her.

"El," she replied, willing the warmth that had pooled in her belly away. "What are you doing here?" Avery gestured to the guard, and waved him off. The burly, six-foot-two man stepped back, giving her and El some space.

"Maybe I just wanted to come and see for myself if you were real. Or if you were a figment of my imagination."

The barb hurt, but she didn't blame him. The last time they'd seen each other hadn't been pleasant. In fact, she'd rate it as one of the worst moments of her life. Three years hadn't been long enough to erase the hurt or the longing she felt simply being in his presence.

Massaging her aching temple, she answered, "Touché."

They stood in silence, each of them taking the other in. His gaze traveled down the length of her body, causing the hairs on her arms to stand on end and her stomach to do the crazy flips it always had when he was near. Like a magnet, his pull made her want to step forward, right into his arms. She wouldn't, of course. Too much had happened between them to ever go there again.

"Are you okay?" he asked, concern now shining in his dark orbs. "You look like you don't feel well."

"I'm fine," she lied, knowing he wouldn't believe her. He'd always been able to see right through her. *Except the one time he didn't.*

"Good speech," he told her.

"Thanks. I was nervous."

"I couldn't tell."

This wasn't right. Awkward conversation wasn't something she'd ever have associated with the two of them. Not even on the day they met had their conversation consisted of averted gazes and start–stops.

"Why did you really come, El?"

His tongue darted out to wet his lips and she followed the motion intently. "Honestly, I don't know. I heard you were asked to give the keynote speech, and I know it's something you've always wanted to do. I guess I was just curious, interested in hearing what you had to say."

"Well?"

He edged closer to her. "You said exactly what I thought you'd say."

Avery sucked in a deep breath when he inched even closer. Swallowing, she croaked, "And what's that?"

He shrugged. "Be open to possibilities. I wonder, though…" He brushed a hair off her forehead. His touch was feather soft, yet Avery felt like he was winding her up, pulling her at all ends.

She wasn't sure what he was about, but she needed to do something, say something, that would put them back on an even footing. Because right then he was in control and she was…wanting him to be in control—of her body and her mind. The thought was sobering, considering it had been several years since they'd even conversed. El was still the only man who had that effect on her.

"What do you wonder?" she asked, leaning forward against her better judgment.

Sighing, El glanced at his phone. "Nothing."

Avery knew El well enough to know that whatever he'd been going to say would never be said. And she just had to be okay with that.

She allowed herself another glance at his tall, lean frame, his brown skin and curly mane. Everything about him was still perfect. She glanced at his wrist and her heart swelled.

"You're wearing the watch I gave you," she said, changing the subject.

El shrugged. "I'm not even sure why. It's just a reminder of the time we've been apart."

Avery remembered that Christmas morning, waking up next to him after making love all night. She recalled how excited he'd been when he opened the gift. The Banneker watch was made using luxury wood, but she knew the significance of the timepiece would mean more to El than the watch itself. That was why she'd saved up and purchased it for him. Banneker Inc. was a minority-owned watch and clock company, named after African American scientist Benjamin Banneker. It was also one of the only watch companies operated by people of color. Each watch was original and the packaging included information about Benjamin Banneker's many accomplishments.

Avery smiled sadly. "El, I guess I understand why you feel the way you do, but can we—"

The loud blare of his phone interrupted her attempt to…what? Talk? Make amends? Start over? At this point, she wasn't sure what she wanted.

El turned his back on her as he answered his phone. The low, serious tone of his voice told her it was the hospital. Her speculations were confirmed when he turned around and told her, "I have to go."

Before she could stop him, he disappeared around the corner.

When she arrived back at the hotel, she pulled her suit coat off and kicked her shoes off. Usually there was a flurry of activity around her at all times, but the suite was relatively quiet, which was exactly what she needed. She'd only been in Michigan for a few hours and it already felt like a lifetime.

Although Ann Arbor was her home for most of her life, it had been months since she'd been back. The last visit was incognito. She'd flown in for a family funeral and left again before the day was out. It

wasn't that she hated her city. It was just the opposite. Even though Avery now called Georgia home,
as beautiful and happening as Atlanta was, it paled
in comparison to her hometown and her home state
in her mind. She'd often dreamed of the tree-lined
streets, colorful people and Blimpy burgers. But life
had taken her in a different direction—away from
everything she'd thought she held dear, including El.
Her town had been good to her today, though. The
temperature was a comfortable seventy-five degrees,
with a light wind and blue skies. It was a beautiful
May day, one she wished she could have enjoyed.

"Avery?"

The familiar voice of her best friend called to her,
jolting her out of her memories. "Jess? You're here?
Yay!" Avery embraced her friend Jessica Brown in
a tight hug. "I thought I was going to see you at the
graduation."

"I know. I tried to get there," Jess said. "My meeting ran longer than I thought it would."

Avery waved her friend off. "It's okay. That, I
definitely understand."

Work was always hectic for Avery, and it seemed
her life was one big meeting. If she wasn't imple-
menting last minute script changes with her staff,
meeting with network executives or running from
one interview to the next, she was writing until the
wee hours of the morning.

"No worries," Avery told Jess. "You can probably
watch it on YouTube right now."

Jess eyed her. "Avery?"

"Huh?" she answered, squeezing her eyes shut.
The headache that she'd woken up with that morn-

ing had seemed to intensify after her run-in with El. However, there was no time built into her schedule for sickness. Unfortunately, no amount of pain reliever seemed to ease the symptoms. Massaging her temples, she met her friend's cautious gaze. "I've missed you, girlfriend. We all set for the flight? I'm so glad you're coming to LA with me."

Jess nodded, concern in her dark-brown eyes. "Yes, but are you okay? You don't look well."

"Avery!"

Her attention snapped to Luke, her assistant. *So much for quiet.* Luke had been with her for the past year, and he'd definitely made the job his own with his exceptional ability to multitask and keep her on time. Avery had a tendency to get so engrossed in work that she forgot to do simple things, like eat or shower or sleep. He'd insisted on traveling with her to Ann Arbor so they could finalize her summer schedule before he left for his month-long vacation back home in Alaska. A last-minute trip to Los Angeles to film a segment on a popular morning talk show was her last appearance. Then Avery was also finally taking some time off. "Yes, Luke."

Luke was scribbling wildly in his planner, his bald head gleaming. "Walter called. He wants to know if you can squeeze in a—"

"No," Avery told him. "I told you, I wanted this time to work on something personal for me."

"I'll let him know," Luke grumbled. "Oh, Monique has called several times. I told her you'd get back with her as soon as possible."

Avery groaned and took a seat on a sofa. Monique was one of her scriptwriters who was more than likely calling about the new changes Avery sent earlier that morning. "I know, Luke. Trust me, I know."

When Avery submitted the novel she'd written in her spare time during a summer break to a publisher all those years ago, she had no idea the world she'd created would eventually turn into the wildly successful drama series *The Preserves*. One day she'd been in her fourth year of medical school and finishing a yearlong master's degree in clinical research, the next she'd been "discovered" and eventually transformed into an overnight celebrity. Who knew a collection of stories based on the neighborhood she'd grown up in would be this popular? So popular that her little book was optioned for a scripted television series that had recently finished its first season a ratings hit. There were chat rooms devoted to her, fan fiction created around her characters and her world.

Luke strutted over and set a piece of paper in front of her. "According to Monique, the network doesn't like the direction you're going for next season. They want changes. You may have to rethink the love triangle. The audience is too invested in Robert and Riley. We can't throw Caleb into the mix."

Scanning the document Luke handed her—a screen print of the first page of her new script— she frowned at the word "No" in big bold letters across the top of the paper. *Damn.* "Get Walter on the phone," she ordered, sighing heavily. "Tell him to handle it. It's his job to go to bat for me with the network. I can't do this right now."

Jess set a tall glass of ice water in front of her, and Avery gulped it down in two-point-two seconds.

Something wasn't right, but she couldn't put her finger on it. Swallowing roughly, she closed her eyes and briefly considered calling her doctor.

"Luke," Avery called out, without opening her eyes. "Leave. You have a plane to catch. I'll be fine. Jess is rolling with me while you're out."

Avery intended to return to Michigan after her trip to Los Angeles to work on her special project, the Avery Montgomery Foundation. Although Avery was sure she could handle her life without Luke, Jess had agreed to step in and help when she could, if things went left.

Avery's competent but loud assistant announced a few last-minute changes to her LA itinerary, and within ten minutes he was gone.

Now alone with Jess, Avery let out a slow breath. Peace and quiet was what she needed.

"So, how did the speech go?" Jess asked, joining her on the sofa. "Did you get a chance to meet any of the… Avery?"

Avery couldn't think. It made her head throb even more.

"Avery," Jess whispered, pressing a comforting hand to her back. "Maybe you should lie down."

Avery shook her head. "I'm fine, so stop worrying."

"But…" Jess shrugged. "I'll grab you something to eat. Maybe that will help."

Avery was excited to spend some time with her best friend. She appreciated Jess more than the other woman would probably ever know.

Avery was the youngest of five. Her father had married her mother after a nasty divorce from his first wife. Her siblings were all at least a decade older than she, which had made for a lonely childhood at times. More than that, her older sisters couldn't stand her because she represented the deterioration of their parents' relationship. They also couldn't stand Avery's mother, Janice, so her sisters had never really tried to have a relationship with her. Despite how often she'd tried to reach out to them, they never reciprocated and she'd eventually given up.

But Jess had filled in the gaps, becoming the sister she'd always dreamed she'd have in her own sisters. Their bond had never dissipated, even though they'd found themselves pulled in different directions. Avery had been hell-bent on becoming a doctor, while Jess had her heart set on becoming an educator. Yet even though they'd run in different school crowds, they'd still managed to stay close. Avery had stood up at Jess's wedding as her maid of honor. And when Jess lost her husband to a horrible accident mere weeks after her wedding, Avery had dropped everything to support her.

In recent years, Jess had turned her focus to empowering high school students hoping to attend the University of Michigan. As Director of Academic Success at the Ross Business School, Jess had been transforming lives and increasing African American enrollment at the college.

They'd saved each other countless times over the years, and Avery wouldn't trade her friendship with Jess for anything or anyone.

Avery wanted to confess to her friend about El. Lord knew she needed to tell someone. But she didn't want to hear what would inevitably come next. Jess wouldn't be able to help herself. The other woman was firmly #TeamEl, and it would undoubtedly piss Avery off. The last thing she wanted to hear was her bestie waxing poetic about signs and connections and meant-to-be romance. That heartwarming love stuff was for romance novels. Avery's life consisted of the heavy drama, lies and sex she had to dream up so that the viewers could get their dose on every Wednesday at eight o'clock. Yeah, no. She'd keep it to herself.

A tingling in her arm had her shaking it furiously in the air. She stood abruptly and swayed on her feet. When she took a step, a wave of dizziness stopped her in her tracks. She gripped the edge of the table.

I can do this, she told herself as she shuffled toward the bedroom. She had to be on her way to Detroit Metropolitan Airport within the hour in order to make the flight to LA.

"Have you thought about the position the school offered?" Jessica asked. "I think it's a wonderful opportunity."

"I thought about it, but it's just not going to work for me."

The University of Michigan had offered Avery an associate professor position in the Master of Fine Arts in Creative Writing program when she'd arrived that morning. Although the idea was appealing on some level, she had no intention of taking it. With her hectic work schedule and establishing her foundation, it just wasn't possible to add anything else to her plate. Besides, moving back to Ann Arbor at this stage in her career wasn't an option for her, especially since her production company was based in Atlanta.

"I can't take on anything else," she continued. "Especially since I'm ready to hit 'play' on the Avery Montgomery Foundation we talked about."

The paperwork had already been done and filed to start the nonprofit. But due to deadlines and shooting, Avery hadn't been able to work on it.

Jess's eyes lit up with excitement. "That's wonderful. I'm so excited."

One of Avery's bucket list items included a foundation to help young girls fund and survive college. Although Avery had decided to go in a different direction, career-wise, the world needed more women in fields like molecular biology or biophysics. There were so many gifted young girls who wanted to attend college, but sometimes the lack of money—especially the prospect of overwhelming student loan debt—made it impossible for them to follow that dream.

Leaning against the wall, Avery sighed. "I'm going to need your help, Jess. This is huge. I purposely scheduled my vacation here so that I can get this going. I want Ann Arbor to be the home base for this project. When we get back from LA, I'm ready to hit the ground running on this, before shooting starts and I have to go back to Atlanta."

"But wouldn't it make sense to just cancel LA, rest a few days before you jump into this? You've been running too long and too hard, Avery. You can't do everything. I worry about you."

Avery smiled. "Don't worry. I'll have time to rest."

As Avery neared the suite's bedroom, she felt herself losing her balance. Forging ahead, she reached the threshold of the separate sleeping area and leaned against the door. Sucking in a deep breath, she glanced at her watch.

Jess's voice was soft in her ear. "I can order you cottage cheese and crackers. Do you want tea?"

Shaking her head, she blinked up at Jessica. Only she couldn't see her friend's face. The only thing she saw was Jess's eye. Panic welled up inside Avery. "Jess?"

"Yes?"

"I can't see you." Avery closed her eyes, then opened them again. There it was again. Jessica's eye. "Seriously. I can't see you."

"Avery, that doesn't make any sense. I'm right in front of you."

"I know that," Avery snapped. "Don't you think I know that? I saw you a minute ago, and now I can't see you. It's like… I don't know. My sight is gone."

"We need to call the doctor," Jessica said. "This isn't normal."

"Wait." Avery closed her eyes. "No, I don't have time to go see a doctor. There's too much to do."

"Avery, I think we should call El—"

"Hell, no. No way."

"He's on staff. He would know someone who can help?"

Sure, El worked at the university hospital, and so did most of his family of doctors, but she couldn't see him again so soon. Their little encounter earlier had been painful enough. Hell, it was torture just thinking about him. It was better if she kept her distance.

Elwood was, for all intents and purposes, the love of her life. But she'd chosen to walk away from him. Their breakup had played out in such a way that had made him think she'd chosen her burgeoning writing career and the prospect of fame over him. Well, that's essentially what he'd accused her of in the months after they split up. He had no idea that leaving him behind was the hardest decision she'd ever made, and being around him again would only open that wound.

El didn't know the real reason she'd left him. He didn't know that his brother, Dr. Lawrence Jackson, had played on her insecurities and she'd let him. She'd allowed another person to get into her head, to convince her that she wasn't good enough, cultured enough, for El. In the end, she'd walked away from her heart because she'd actually believed it, and that was the greatest tragedy of all.

Finally opening her eyes again, she was mortified to find that she still couldn't see more than Jess's eye, but she kept her mouth shut. If she told her best friend, there was no way she'd be able to talk Jess out of calling 911.

The room swirled around her, and she let out a slow, shaky breath. "Jess?"

Then everything went black.

Chapter 2

Elwood wasn't a glutton for punishment. Usually he didn't willingly put himself in harm's way or make rash decisions that would affect his emotional well-being. He was a paid therapist, a medical doctor of psychiatry. It was his job to see to the mental welfare of his patients, to help them stabilize their symptoms. But this time…he'd purposefully done something that would no doubt interrupt his sleep for the next few days.

El jumped up and paced the confines of his office. Going to the Power Center just to get a glimpse of Avery had been the wrong move. He'd known it when he used a break in his schedule to leave the hospital, to walk the short distance to the campus auditorium. Along the way, he'd reasoned with himself on the whys. Why did he feel the need to see her? Why would this time be any different from their last encounter? Why couldn't he get over her?

That last question had almost made him turn around in his tracks and abort the mission. Yet he'd kept going, using the nice weather as an excuse to propel himself forward. When he'd arrived—late— Avery was at the end of her speech. She'd obviously done a fabulous job as the standing-room-only auditorium was full of people laughing and crying and clapping.

When she'd faltered on stage, he'd known immediately that his entrance hadn't been as subtle as he'd hoped. How she'd seen him in the sea of faces was beyond him, but he'd figured it was just the way it had always been. Like moths to a flame, when one of them was near the other, there was no way to stop the pull.

What he hadn't planned on was his need to confront her. Well, *confront* was the wrong word. He needed to see for himself if she was still as beautiful as he'd remembered, if she still smelled like jasmine and orchids. Up close and personal, she was as breathtaking as a sunset over white beach sand with her topaz eyes, smooth mocha skin and pouty lips. Her signature flowing mane had been trimmed into a chin-length bob, but it was still the color of molasses. If he'd dared to step closer, he knew she'd fit right in the nook of his arms, snugly under his chin.

El knew that if he closed his eyes right then, he'd see her, hear her soft voice and feel her lips against his. It was his most vivid fantasy, almost as if she'd set up permanent residence in his thoughts and dreams. It didn't matter who he was with—and he'd made it a full-time job to get over her—she was the woman he longed for.

Thoughts like those often gave him pause when he thought of Avery. She was goal-oriented, driven to the point of madness at times. But then she could be sweet, docile even. It had been those times—when she was only his, when there was no pressure from the world she'd created in her head or the demands of her career—that made him love her even more.

The knock on his office door jolted El out of his head, for which he was grateful. Enough of the *Avery* haze.

His administrative assistant, Sophie, poked her head into his office. "Dr. Jackson, you have a visitor."

Elwood nodded. "Who is it?"

"It's me, Unc," Drake said, pushing past Sophie. "I've been trying to call you all day. Let's grab dinner."

Ignoring his nephew, El smiled at Sophie. "Thanks, Sophie. You can leave for the day. Thanks for staying late."

Sophie gave him a quick summary of his early morning schedule the next day, reminded him that she had a doctor's appointment in the morning and would be late, then excused herself.

"I need a Sophie for my office," Drake admitted, taking a seat on the couch intended for El's patients. "What are you thinking for dinner?"

El leaned back in his chair and stared at his not-that-much-younger nephew. He hated when Drake called him *Unc*. At age thirty-five, El was only a few years older than Drake. They were more like brothers, than uncle and nephew.

"Do you always think about food?" El asked. "The

only reason you're here is because Love is out of town." Drake's wife, Dr. Lovely Grace Washington-Jackson, had been gone for a week and El had been forced to entertain his nephew every night. Even if he'd had a woman waiting in the wings, his nephew had made player hating his *modus operandi* for the week. "Maybe you need to take a cooking class so that you can make your own dinner when your wife is not available."

"Hey, you need some laughter in your life," Drake countered. "If it weren't for me, you'd be sitting here at the hospital every night, charting and listening to yourself talk into that damn recorder."

Drake had been insisting that El go out with Love's cousin Lana. The sneaky matchmaking couple had blatantly set up numerous dinners under the guise of fake celebrations, like Love almost being pregnant or Drake successfully operating on a patient. Not that he didn't hope Love would realize her dream of being a mother or that he wasn't proud of his nephew's impressive surgical record. But every single thing that happened didn't need to be celebrated with dinner and drinks at a high-brow restaurant downtown.

"You don't know my life, Drake. And I'd appreciate it if you didn't act like you did."

Drake shrugged. "I'm just sayin'. If I don't tell you the truth, who will?"

"How about you concentrate on your life with your beautiful wife. Leave my business to me."

It was no use telling Drake to mind his own business. He'd learned early on that he had no private business growing up in a house with the younger Jacksons.

Drake was the eldest son of El's brother, the incomparable plastic surgeon Dr. Lawrence Jackson. Behind Drake were the twins, Ian and Myles. His sweet niece, Melanie, came later.

When El was five years old, Lawrence took him in and raised him along with his own children. Lawrence was twenty-one years older, and El was the "oopsie" baby, an unplanned inconvenience to his parents, who'd preferred to hire nannies than spend quality time with him.

Before his brother rescued him, El's childhood had been cold, a web of loneliness and despair. His mother and father had barely spared him a glance, and when they did it was to tell him that he was a mistake they didn't want.

Once El left his parents' home, he'd never looked back or even communicated with them again. He couldn't even bring himself to attend their funerals. As far as he was concerned, they didn't deserve to be anyone's parents.

Most often, his brother wasn't known for his kindness, but that one decision had changed El's life for the better. And despite Lawrence's many flaws, inherited from their parents, El would always be grateful to his brother for stepping in.

El met Drake's intent gaze. "What?" he asked.

Drake assessed him, a frown deepening on his brow. "You went to the Power Center, didn't you?"

El stood up. "Are you ready to go? Thai?"

Drake stood, but made no move toward the door.

"You did. You went to see Avery at the Black Celebratory."

El closed his laptop and shoved it into his bag. As if Drake wasn't standing there watching his every move, he continued to pack up his belongings. He'd finish working at home.

"How did she look?" Drake asked.

When he met his nephew's gaze, he couldn't ignore the gleam in Drake's eyes. "Damn good," he admitted finally. "She was still Avery."

Drake barked out a laugh. "I knew you wouldn't be able to resist. I always told you that you let her go too easily, but you're too damn stubborn to admit it."

"I thought I was the psychiatrist in the family. You stick to cardiothoracic surgery, and stop trying to figure me out."

"Did you talk to her?"

El zipped up his messenger bag. "I did."

"Well?" Drake asked after a few seconds.

"Well, nothing. She is still Avery, busy and about *her* business."

The sarcasm in his words wasn't lost on his nephew, who folded his arms across his chest and planted himself on the arm of a chair.

"Drake, I don't want to talk about her," El persisted. "I went to see her. We had words. I left. Nothing more, nothing less. Let's go."

Except, El knew there was more to that visit than he'd let on to Drake.

"How long will she be here?" Drake stood up and walked toward the door. "I want to see her."

"I have no idea." They left his office and headed toward the elevators. "I had to use the emergency room valet when I came back." El had been called back to the hospital earlier when one of his patients attempted suicide, and had never gotten a chance to move his car.

They fell into step beside each other as they walked to the Emergency Department parking lot.

A few people breezed past them as they neared the doors. El noted the crowd in the waiting room.

"Are those photographers?" Drake asked, pointing toward the glass doors at the entrance.

El frowned. Photographers in the ER were a rare occurrence, and he wondered what had happened. He caught a glimpse of the same guard he'd seen earlier with Avery as the burly man stormed into the triage area.

When he saw a distraught Jessica run in next, his heart fell. Because on the gurney behind Jess was Avery.

Drake jumped into action first, calling Avery's name as he met the paramedics. Shock, fear and concern shot through El at the sight of an unconscious Avery. The paramedics yelled out commands, while Drake barked out a few of his own.

"El?" Drake barked. "Snap out of it."

El peered down at Avery, then at Jess. "What happened?" he shouted.

Jess was barely holding on. Her eyes were swollen and red, and pieces of tissue were stuck to her cheek. "She…" she croaked, swallowing visibly. "I knew she didn't feel well. I told her to rest, but she wouldn't. El, what if she dies?"

El grabbed Jess's shoulders and squeezed gently. "She won't die, but I need you to tell me what happened."

El prided himself on being able to hear two conversations at once. It often came in handy in his line of work. He was able to talk to Jess and hear the symptoms being thrown out by the medical personnel working on Avery. *Vision changes and high blood pressure.* Jess continued her explanation, telling El about Avery's behavior after the graduation. *Severe headache.* The other woman explained that Avery told her she couldn't see her. *Possible stroke.*

Possible stroke? He turned to Drake. "What?" he asked.

Drake lowered his head. "It sounds like it."

Before El could ask anything else, emergency room staff were there, pulling Avery behind the frosted glass. Drake was right behind them, dialing furiously on his phone.

Jess tried to push her way through, but El held her back. "Jess, you can't go back there."

"But she needs me," Jess yelled, panic in her voice. "I can't leave her alone."

"She'll be fine. Let the doctors do their job."

El couldn't believe how easily the words came out. Sure, he'd practiced them thousands of times in medical school. When there was nothing else left to say, encourage the family to let the doctors do their job. Only this wasn't a random patient; it was Avery, the only woman he'd ever loved. And she was fighting for her life.

Hours later, an ER doctor pulled some strings and El and Jess were allowed in the room while the doctors worked on Avery. Drake had been called away for an emergency, but had been checking in periodically.

It was surreal to see his colleagues, some of his friends, working on Avery. Many of them had attended college with them, had known her before she was *the* Avery Montgomery who had a hit television show on network television. Of course, they were professional, but occasionally one of them would shoot him a sad glance. A few would give him updates as they worked.

Avery Montgomery was high profile, and the hospital had taken steps to secure the facility so that they could save her life without interruptions. Only a few people were allowed on the hidden floor where they'd taken her. It hadn't stopped the phone from ringing. Jess had two, and had been frantically barking orders over the lines. Each call had seemed to fray Jess's nerves even more, and he'd finally convinced her to hand over the devices to him.

El had managed to get Jess to settle down, but every few minutes she would break down in a fit of tears. This time Jess was bent over, shaking, as a sob broke through the activity in the room.

He rubbed her back. "Jess, she's going to beat this."

His words were meant to soothe Jess, calm her. But they weren't just for her benefit. They were for his, as well.

She peered up at him and offered him a watery smile. "What if she doesn't?"

"Don't say that," he snapped, before he was able to catch himself.

"I told her to cancel the trip to LA, to rest. She

just didn't look good. I know her, had a feeling she'd forgotten to eat."

El chuckled. "I remember. That woman never took care of herself. I had to make her drink a protein shake or eat an apple when she was working in the lab."

Jessica shook her head. "When she came back from the graduation she was distracted, but I could tell she was battling something."

El couldn't help the guilt that crept in at Jessica's admission.

"I told her to lie down before we went to the airport," she continued. "El, watching my best friend collapse into a seizure was the worst thing I've ever witnessed."

He was at a loss for words. El knew that was saying a lot for Jess, considering her husband had died a few years earlier.

Shaking her head, Jess finished her bottled water. "It was awful. And I feel so bad that I didn't believe her at first. I thought she was joking."

"Don't do that to yourself. You couldn't have known."

The doctors had told him and Jess that Avery had a stroke that affected her vision and caused her to lose her sight earlier when she was with Jess. According to the attending physician, surgery wasn't needed, which was a relief to El. Yet there was no way to tell if the damage was permanent at that point, since Avery was still unconscious. El could only pray that it wasn't, because if Avery lost her sight forever, it would destroy her.

Chapter 3

Where am I? Avery heard voices, but they weren't familiar. They were detached, stiff. Doctors? She tried to open her eyes, tried to speak, but the words wouldn't come. She tried to open her eyes, but darkness surrounded her.

"Avery?" Jess's voice in her ear immediately calmed her.

"Jess," Avery muttered with a cough.

"I'm here," her friend said. "You're at the University hospital. You had us worried sick."

Why?

Avery remembered the graduation, being face-to-face with El and the hotel room. When she felt the flutter of her lashes on her cheeks as she blinked, she realized that her eyes had been open, but she couldn't see.

Fear welled up inside her as she tried to hone in on the sounds and sensations around her—the shrill beeping of machines, the suction of the blood pressure cuff on her arm, the foul, dry taste in her mouth, the medicinal hospital smell. Four of her senses were working, but the one she relied on the most, the one she needed to earn her bread and butter, had failed her.

Closing her eyes, she let a whimper escape and the tears followed shortly after. The muscles in her legs tightened, and the urge to flee took over. But she couldn't move.

Avery felt Jess's hand rubbing her arm, and she reached out to hold on to it with her other hand. Squeezing tightly, she said, "Please tell me this isn't permanent. What's wrong with me?"

Her voice sounded desperate to her own ears and she wondered who was in the room with her. She had to assume there were people she knew in the room with her, people with whom she'd attended medical school, but she still hadn't recognized any of the voices.

"Calm down, hun," Jess whispered. "Your blood pressure is spiking again."

Avery gasped, expelling a ragged breath. It hurt to breathe. It hurt to think. "Blood pressure. Why?"

"You had a stroke. The doctors think it was caused by high blood pressure brought on by continued stress. The scans indicate you have blood on the brain."

Avery knew what that meant. Years of studying to become a doctor hadn't left her. Vision changes brought on by a stroke were hard to overcome. The likelihood of regaining her sight was low, rare. Squeezing her eyes closed, she couldn't hold it back any longer. She sobbed openly, screamed loudly, drowning out everything around her. It was an uncontrollable, ugly cry. In that moment, she didn't care who heard her. Nothing mattered, not appearances, not her pride.

Jess held her, rubbed her back and murmured words of encouragement in her ear. "Oh, hun, I'm here. I won't leave. You can depend on me."

"What am I going to do?" Avery cried. "How am I—?" She choked as the tears continued to flow.

"Avery?"

Avery froze. Turning her head to his voice, she called his name. "El?"

"Yes," he said. His calm voice soothed like balm to an open wound.

"You're here?" It wasn't a question. Well, at least, she hadn't intended it to be.

She reached out and within a few seconds she felt the stubble on his chin. She inhaled the lingering scent of his cologne, let the notes of sage, lavender and mandarin ease her mind. Her fingers traced the outline of his forehead, felt the frown lines on his forehead. She brushed the line of his nose and ran her thumb over his full lips.

She smelled the hazelnut on his breath, felt it against her cheek as he leaned in.

"You're okay," he told her. "You're going to be just fine."

Her first response to his words was to nod in agreement. Because, for some reason, she believed him. Logically, she knew the odds, but El had a way of making her believe almost anything.

The press of his forehead against her temple made her turn her head toward him. She needed a deeper connection to him in that moment. The tips of his fingers brushed the outline of her ear and she savored the touch.

The tenderness he showed her, despite everything she'd put him through, was enough to make her belly ache with yearning. He'd known what she needed right then. He always knew how to take the pain away, if only for a brief moment. When the warmth of his mouth pressed against her forehead, she held her breath and let the flutter in her stomach take over.

His proximity, his presence, was what she needed to handle the shock of her trauma. Vaguely she felt moisture drizzle down the arm Jess was holding. Her poor friend was probably a nervous wreck. Avery had to be strong. She had to figure out her next steps.

"I need answers," Avery said, sucking in all of her emotions. Her question wasn't directed to anyone specific, though. She sensed the quiet presence of many people in the room and she wanted to know the extent of the damage.

"It was a hemorrhagic stroke that accompanied the onset of hypertensive encephalopathy. Your body couldn't take the sudden increase in your blood pressure," a strange voice explained. She assumed it was a doctor. "Ms. Montgomery, my name is Dr. Thorne. I'm the neuro-ophthalmologist assigned to your case. I've been briefed on your history and your knowledge of medicine, so I'll be candid. As you know, it's too soon to ascertain if your sight will return. But based on the latest scans, there is a good chance it will."

Avery closed her eyes and said a silent prayer to God for healing.

"Avery?" El called. "We're all here to help. There is more testing to be done, but I'm going to need you to hold it together. We can't afford another spike in your blood pressure right now. I know you're scared, but try to relax and let them do their work."

El then introduced her to every other physician in the room. Some she knew and some she didn't. He must've informed them all of her background, because they spoke to her in a language only used among one of their own. Once she'd received the updates, she opened her eyes.

It wasn't a dream. She still couldn't see a damn thing. She darted her eyes back and forth, hoping something would give. No faces, nothing—until the glint of metal flashed into her view. It was small, but she immediately knew what it was. It was the metal on El's watch—the watch she'd given him.

A tear slid down her cheek, and it startled her because she hadn't realized she was crying again. She felt the pad of El's thumb sweep across her face, then felt a soft tissue against her skin. Her emotions were all over the place but she knew she couldn't afford to let them get the best of her. She needed to get through this so she could go back to her life. As soon as possible.

Later, after countless scans, multiple blood draws and too many neurological exams, Avery was over it. Everything in her wanted to blow up, yell at everyone within earshot. She'd done just that a little over an hour ago, taking no prisoners, and she didn't even care if she'd hurt feelings.

Avery shook her head, lifting her chin high in the air. As she grew more restless, she felt her muscles quiver and her pulse speed up. Heat flushed through her body, straight to her toes. The despair she'd felt when she woke up surrounded by doctors, the slight hope she'd felt earlier when El was in the room, had been eclipsed by the fear she'd tried to trick away. And when Avery was scared, she became angry and irritable. Seeing the glint of El's watch had been an isolated incident, a fluke, because the darkness seemed never ending. She'd yet to see anything, not even a flash of light.

She was too young, too busy, too smart for this. It wasn't rocket science. She'd read all the textbooks, studied the medicine in school. She worked out regularly, ate healthy foods—when she remembered to eat. *What the hell?*

As the cuff on her arm tightened uncomfortably, she squirmed in the bed. If she'd been able to see, she would have been out of there with "the quickness," as they used to say back in the day. A nurse announced her vital signs and gave her a few pills. She didn't ask what pills they were. She didn't even care. She just wanted to feel better.

Her life wasn't going to stop because she'd had a stroke. *Who has a stroke at thirty-two years of age anyway?* The network was probably calling, wondering why she wasn't in LA, wondering where her script edits were for the second season premiere.

"Getting angry isn't going to help."

Avery jumped at the sound of El's voice, coming

from the far left of the room. What was he doing there? She'd asked to be alone, even sent the reluctant Jess home to get rest. "Why are you here?" she growled. "Get out!"

She heard the click of his heels against the floor, but instead of heading toward the door, the steps grew closer to the bed. Then there was nothing. He was still there, though—watching her, assessing her like he undoubtedly did with his patients.

"What do you want from me?" she demanded. "We're not together anymore. That was *my* choice for a reason. You don't have to be here, and I don't want you here."

It was the first time she'd felt glad she couldn't see his face. Her words had to have stung, and she didn't want to see the evidence of that truth in his eyes. Most of all, she didn't want him to see her like this, wounded and angry. Because for all of her bravado earlier, for all of her positive thoughts about her life not stopping because of this new development, she was a wrecking ball of emotion. She'd made a good living using her eyes, and knowing that there was a chance she'd never be able to see again ripped her to shreds. The only thing she wanted in that moment was to be alone so that no one could see her torment.

"You don't have to pretend to care, El," she added. "You made it perfectly clear at the auditorium that you still harbor resentment toward me for following *my* dreams instead of attaching myself to your coattails."

When he didn't respond or even make a sound of acknowledgment, she let out a shaky breath and tried to burrow her body into the bed.

"Please, go," she pleaded, her chin trembling. "I'm fine here."

"You really get on my nerves," he said finally, with a chuckle. "Your damn mouth always got you into trouble."

Avery's mouth fell open, then closed again. She couldn't even respond to that because she knew it to be true. Even as a child, it had kept her in trouble with her parents. Strong willed, stubborn, whatever you wanted to call it. She was the reason her mother went gray at forty-five.

"I knew the anger would come, Avery," he said. "It always does when you're scared. I just wanted to be here when you let it take over, to make sure you got it out and let it go."

I hate you.

"I'm sure you do," he countered, to her horror. She hadn't meant to say it out loud.

Avery apologized. "I didn't mean it."

"Yes, you did. In this moment, you probably do hate me. What you said was the absolute truth. I do resent you for leaving the way you did." His confession took her by surprise, but she did her best to not show it. "But you're not going to get better if you keep stressing the way you do. Do you not understand that your blood pressure was so high it caused a neurological crisis in your body? All work, all day, will make Avery a dead woman."

His blunt truth felt like a fist around her heart. El had always told her to slow down, to appreciate life. He'd warned her that her goals were great, but there was only so much she could do in a day. And she hadn't listened. Case in point, she'd been going nonstop for weeks, appearing on late-night television, flying from coast to coast for meetings, answering every single phone call, writing until her fingers cramped up.

She didn't expect him to understand, either. He'd never had to worry about anything. His life was golden, charmed. Born to one of the richest families in Ann Arbor brought automatic approval from the community. Avery had to work for everything she'd ever received. Her parents weren't wealthy. Both of them had worked, from dusk until dawn to make ends meet, to support her.

"No, we aren't a couple anymore," he continued. "But we were friends long before I ever kissed you. As your *friend*, I need you to get it together You've had your angry moment. Don't let it consume you or distract you from the ultimate goal."

Avery rolled her eyes and cursed the traitorous tears that escaped. "And what would that goal be?" The sarcasm dripping from her words was intended to be noticeable.

"Rest. Let your body heal and pray your vision comes back sooner rather than later. Then get the hell out of town. That simple."

"Avery?" Jess said. "Are you okay? El, what happened?"

"Nothing," she heard him say. "I'm going to go. Make sure she stays calm. I'll check in on her later."

His soft, sure steps echoed in the room as he walked toward the door.

"El," she called.

"What, Avery?" He was annoyed. She could always tell when he wanted to throttle her by the way he said her name, each syllable pronounced with curt precision.

"Never mind. 'Bye."

He didn't respond. Instead, she heard the door shut softly and wished she'd kept her big mouth shut for once.

Chapter 4

Avery hated ducks. One of her very first memories was a trip to Disney World with her parents. She had to have been around three years old, but she remembered it like it was yesterday. The Disney characters walking around waving at her, the smell of popcorn, the large rides. She also remembered the moment when she saw Cinderella. The huge castle and the prince meant nothing to her. The entire trip led up to the moment she saw her favorite Disney princess wave at her from the balcony of the castle. It had been the best moment of her life.

Then her world had come crashing down, when not even a day later she was chased by a flock of mallard ducks. The memory was so vivid, she often got chills thinking about it. She'd still been on cloud nine after seeing Cinderella and she was at a pond on the hotel grounds with her cousins. She'd seen the ducks, and thought they were pretty and wanted to play with them because… *Donald Duck was fun. Right*?

Unfortunately, her plans didn't turn out quite like she'd wanted and the cute little birds had turned into ugly little terrors when they'd attacked, chasing her all the way back to the safe arms of her father. Growing up, she'd had many fears—pigeons because they pooped everywhere, bees because they stung, tornadoes because they were big. All of those fears went away, but ducks…she was still scared as hell of the things. She'd never known a fear quite like it until now.

Lying there in the hospital bed, with no sight and no idea who was with her, was scary. But Avery Montgomery wasn't supposed to be afraid of anything. She'd conquered Hollywood, people wanted *her* at their parties, network executives invited *her* to their homes and treated *her* to dinner and drinks at exclusive, five-star restaurants. Before she boarded the plane to Detroit, she'd received notification that *her* show was up for a Black Entertainment Television, or BET, award. And to top off her extraordinary week, her bosses submitted *The Preserves* for Prime Time Emmy consideration for Best Dramatic Television Series.

Avery should have been on cloud nine, celebrating her accomplishments with wine, glitz and glamour, but instead she was stuck in a hospital bed. In Ann Arbor. With no vision. In hindsight, she should have known better than to get excited because, without fail, something always happened to douse her dreams with gasoline and light them with a match.

It had happened with the ducks when she was a kid; it had happened today when she'd stroked out.

Swallowing, Avery tried not to cry again. But when she felt the wetness drizzle down her cheek, she accepted that she'd lost that battle.

"I'm scared," she murmured to anyone and no one.

"I know."

It was Jess. It was always Jess. And Avery was grateful because she had someone by her side. "Thank you for being here."

She heard light footsteps approach the bed and instinctively turned toward them. The good news was that she wasn't completely in the dark. She registered light and could vaguely make out a shadow standing to her left where Jess's voice came from.

"I wouldn't go anywhere, Avery. You have to know that."

Jess was crying. Or had been crying. Avery couldn't see her face, but the soft whisper and tremble in her friend's voice told her so. "Do I look bad? Like, if you didn't know I was blind, could you tell?"

Avery felt the cool tips of Jess's fingers as they laced with hers. Squeezing her hand, Jess told her, "You look beautiful, girlfriend." Jess smoothed a hand down the back of her head. "There. Now your hair is right back in place. I wouldn't be able to tell."

"I hurt El." Avery didn't want to imagine El's face when she'd treated him so horribly earlier. He'd been there to help her, to support her, and she'd told him she hated him. It couldn't be further from the truth.

"El knows you," Jess said. "He's not hurt."

How could she know that? El was a master of the poker face. He was paid to not react, but she knew when things affected him, when he was touched by a patient or devastated by an action. She knew when he was angry. She didn't have to see him to know that he'd been pissed when he left her. After all, he hadn't been back. Granted, it hadn't been long. As far as she could tell, it had only been a few hours since he'd walked out. But it was a few hours too long when she needed him.

"I didn't mean it," Avery said. "I was just frustrated."

El had seen her at her best and at her worst. But she'd tried to never take her irritation with the people in her world out on him. He was too good for that. He'd only ever treated her with respect. He deserved more from her than her wrath.

Drawing her bottom lip between her teeth, she shrugged. No sense in worrying about it. He was gone, and it was just her and Jess. "What am I going to do, Jess?"

"You're going to fight, Avery. This is temporary."

"You don't know that, Jess. I've studied medicine. The doctors don't know. There's no way to know. The longer I'm without sight, the…" Avery couldn't finish the thought. Truth was, most people who lose their vision after a stroke didn't fully regain their sight. Sure, she knew that some stroke survivors did experience some recovery but there was no way to tell if she'd be one of those patients. "What the hell am I going to do?"

Jess sighed. "We're going to do everything we can. Call in specialists, go to OT. There are certain surgeries that can…we can do whatever has to be done."

Avery turned away from the hopefulness in her friend's voice. Closing her eyes, she finally let the sob that had been threatening to break free pierce the air. "I'm a writer. If I wasn't a writer, I'd be a molecular freakin' biologist or a doctor. All require vision. How am I supposed to turn in my scripts? How can I even do the legwork for my foundation? I can't drive, Luke isn't here and you have a job. Tell me how this is going to work, Jess."

The tears were coming faster now. She felt them drizzle down her face to her ears. Even if she wanted to stop crying, she wasn't sure she'd be able to. The sound that tore from her throat was more of a wail, almost as if someone was physically hurting her. Only there was no tactile pain. Everything she felt, the inner turmoil racking her body, was like someone taking a fist and squeezing the life out of her heart. Everything that she'd worked for was on the verge of going up in smoke.

Then Avery felt warmth as Jess wrapped her arms around her and held on tightly, rocking her back and forth, whispering broken words of comfort through her own tears. "Avery, it's going to be alright. I've already talked to my boss. He has granted me additional leave time to stay with you. You're going to be okay. You have to believe that."

Avery didn't have to believe anything. She just wanted to. Jess was the positive one. That positivity had remained even after the death of her husband, her first love. "Jess, I wish I had some of your positivity. But I know science. I know medicine. I breathed both for years. I know cell processes and codes. And I know how to write one hell of a cliffhanger."

What she didn't know was how to maintain her

public persona, keep her job and do it without the world knowing she couldn't see.

"You know the story, Avery. You don't have to see to tell it. I'll help you."

The dread in the pit of her stomach prevented her from smiling, even as her heart welled with love for her bestie. "I know, Jess. You always help me. But you won't be able to do that if you don't get some rest. I thought I told you to go get some rest."

It had to be late, or early the next morning. Hours had passed since the Black Celebratory. And Jess obviously hadn't listened to her when she'd told her to leave.

"And I already told you I'm not leaving you here," Jess countered.

Avery shook her head. "Have you reached my parents?"

"No, not yet. You know your parents don't know how to work the wi-fi. With them being on the ship, I'm betting we won't hear from them until they dock in Seattle."

"It's just as well. Let them enjoy their vacation."

Even though Avery loved her parents dearly and they doted on her, there was really nothing they could do for her. She wanted them to enjoy their anniversary trip, an eleven-day Alaskan cruise. Being married for thirty-five years was nothing to scoff at, and she'd been glad to be able to send them on their dream trip. To see them still in love with each other after all that time warmed Avery's heart.

Phillip and Janice Montgomery had Avery late in life. Neither thought they'd find love again after disastrous first marriages, but they had. They'd mar-

ried, expecting to travel the world but...*surprise!*
Avery had been the unexpected wrench in their plans.
Yet they'd never made her feel unwanted. So she'd
made it her mission to give them everything they
wanted. That's why she'd paid off their mortgage
before she even bought herself a home. That's why
she'd always take care of them. Two months ago, her
father celebrated his seventy-fifth birthday and her
mother would turn seventy-one in October. It was
high time for them to enjoy life.

"I'll keep trying," Jess said. "And I'll make sure
they get here. Don't worry."

Avery had finally convinced her parents to move
to Atlanta with her a year ago. Her older siblings
were useless and failed to even call their father to
check on him. She felt better with her mother and
father near her. Of course, they'd insisted on keeping their house in Ann Arbor for when they came
back to visit friends.

"Why don't you go home and sleep in a real bed,
Jess?" Avery knew it would be like pulling teeth to
get her to leave, but she couldn't worry about her
friend getting sick on top of everything else. Jess
suffered from fibromyalgia and needed her sleep. "I
don't want you having a flare-up."

"Avery, I'm fine. So stop telling me to leave because I'm not going anywhere." Avery opened her
mouth to respond, but Jess added, "I will go grab
myself a snack, though, and a cup of coffee. Why
don't you try to get some sleep?"

Nodding, Avery burrowed into the bubble mattress. She felt the compression socks on her legs in-
flate slowly, heard the beep of the machines echoing

in the room and wondered how she was supposed to rest. But she wouldn't argue with Jess.

Jess let out an audible sigh, but seconds later Avery heard the door close. Now alone, Avery swiped an errant tear that escaped and prayed that sleep would come.

When El was a kid, he'd made it a point to stay out of trouble. But it hadn't been because he didn't want to take risks, do things that would possibly land him in a heap of trouble. No, it was because he'd never wanted to rock the boat. He had this incessant need to stay under the radar.

One of the first things he'd learned as an adult, and through his own experience with therapy, was that his need to be invisible was a protection mechanism. It was brought on by his very real fear of being sent back to his parents. He'd lived with Lawrence for two years before he emptied his suitcase. He'd always kept a full suitcase under his bed. Even at five and six years of age.

There was still a part of him that never really felt comfortable in his surroundings, a part of him that never believed he was good enough to love. But that had all changed on a rainy day in April of 2006, the day he met Avery on campus.

El was late and hungry. Unfortunately, the hunger pangs won and he found himself rushing through the Michigan Union toward the Subway restaurant in the MUG. The MUG was the underground food court in the building that housed several restaurants.

As he neared the restaurant, he groaned at the line, but stood at the end anyway. It was taking lon-

ger than usual, but he refused to stand in the even longer line at Wendy's.

The woman in front of him finally stepped up to the counter and placed her order. "I'd like a steak and cheese sub, extra meat, on Italian bread with extra mayo and no veggies," he heard her say.

He let his gaze travel over her petite form and wondered how she maintained her lovely figure with extra steak and extra mayo. For a minute, he thought about saying something to her, but decided to refrain because...well, he didn't know her from Adam.

When the woman slid down the counter, he placed his order. Once at the register, he scowled as the same woman struggled to get exact change from her small wallet.

El muttered a curse and noticed the cashier roll her eyes in frustration. He was tempted to pay for the woman's meal under the guise of "paying it forward," but again refrained from speaking.

A moment later, the woman got her money together, paid for her meal and turned around, giving him a sheepish grin. "I'm sorry," she said. "For holding the line up."

El was speechless. The woman he'd been scowling at was stunning, with her black-rimmed eyeglasses and wavy, natural curls.

His food forgotten, he noted the molecular biology book in her hand. "Who's your professor?"

With a frown on her face, she asked, "Excuse me?"

El grinned, and pointed to her book. "You're taking molecular biology? Who's teaching the class?"

A firm nudge from behind caught him off guard and he practically fell into her. Turning, he glared

*at the person behind him before paying for his own
lunch and grabbing it from the cashier's waiting
hands.*

*A smile spread across the woman's face when his
gaze met hers again. "Professor Luddington," she
answered.*

*Today was his lucky day. "I know her. She's good
people."*

"She's also brutal, but I love the class."

*Intrigued, El smirked. "I don't think I've met any-
one who loves molecular biology."*

*"Well, hello, I'm Avery Montgomery." She held
out her hand to shake his, and he couldn't deny the
heat that passed between them when their palms
touched. "I'm pleased to be the first person you've
ever met that not only loves molecular biology but
plans to graduate at the top of her class with that
major."*

As El walked through the halls on the way to his
office, he remembered their first date, their first kiss,
the first time he'd made love to her. They'd shared
a lot of firsts, but most important was that they'd
been each other's first love. It was a love that was
pure, intense and real. And the passage of time hadn't
changed the depth of his feelings for her. He loved
her, yes. But his anger with her hadn't diminished,
either. That was the problem, because he knew she
needed him. How could he help her when he wanted
to simultaneously punish her for hurting him and
make love to her until all she felt was him?

"El?"

Jarred from his thoughts, he turned to see Jess
standing before him, a cup of coffee in her hand.

"You're back?" Jess asked. "Why didn't you come in?"

El blinked and glanced back at the door he'd been standing in front of. He hadn't realized he'd walked to Avery's room and not his office.

"What's up, Jess?" He gave her a tight hug. "I would ask why you're not asleep, but I already know why."

Jess offered him a weak smile, but no response. El knew Jess recognized his attempt to change the subject and was grateful she hadn't called him on it.

Looking at the petite woman in front of him, he noted that Jess looked…tired. Her once-bright eyes were dimmed, hollow. "You need to rest," he told her.

Ducking her head, Jess ran her thumbnail over the rim of her cup. "I know."

"You won't be any good to her if you're lying in a hospital bed right next to her."

El considered Jess his friend. The two had forged an enduring friendship when he was with Avery. He'd learned that they were a package deal early on in his relationship with Avery. And he hadn't begrudged that. After all, his nephews and niece were just as important to him. Any woman he dated would have to get along with them.

"She's finally sleeping, so I figured I'd take a walk. Can we talk?" Jess asked.

El nodded and led Jess over to the family waiting room down the hall. "How is she?" he asked, taking a seat on an arm of one of the couches.

Jess sighed, traced the bottom of her cup with her thumb, but she remained standing. "I'm worried. There's a lot going on with her."

"That's vague." El wasn't surprised that Jess

hadn't said anything more, but he was genuinely curious about what "a lot" meant.

"Purposefully, because that's not what I wanted to talk to you about."

"Ah. Well, you know you can talk to me about anything. What is it?"

Jess stared straight ahead, as if she was trying to find the right words that wouldn't betray Avery's trust. He sensed she needed to get some things out, so he sat quietly beside her. When he noticed a tear slide down her cheek, he grabbed her hand and squeezed.

Letting out a shaky breath, she said, "I need you to help me help her."

El closed his eyes and let out a deep breath. "I don't think—"

"El, please." Jess tugged at his hand until he opened his eyes. "Please. You can get through to her. She's so scared."

"Well, she's suffered a trauma, Jess. That's normal."

"You know as well as I do that Avery is used to being the one in control. She doesn't do well with fear. I know she hurt you, but you have to know that it was the fear talking."

El met Jess's gaze, but he didn't respond. Yes, Avery had lashed out, but he wasn't hurt. Irritated, yes. Hurt, no. "That's not true. That little tiff in the hospital room was expected. I wasn't hurt."

"That's not what I'm talking about, and you know it."

"Jess, this is not up for discussion. Avery was not scared when she ended things with me."

El tried to rein in his anger, shake the ice out of his veins. Even now, the thought of that day, the hour, the very minute she'd broken up with him, made him cold.

Avery had ripped him to shreds when she'd left with the flimsiest of explanations. When she'd told him that an agent wanted to represent her to sell her book, he'd been happy for her. When she'd told him that said agent had sold her book at auction for a six-figure advance, he'd been elated. When she'd explained that she needed to drop out of medical school, he'd supported her. Even when she'd mentioned living in Atlanta, he was good with it, knowing he'd move heaven and earth to make it work.

And for a while it did. They'd visited each other on weekends, called each other every night. Then something changed and suddenly their long-distance relationship hadn't worked for her anymore. *He* hadn't worked for her anymore.

Then "Hollywood" came calling and it was over. It hadn't mattered how many answers he'd demanded, how willing he'd been to try—she'd shut him down. Years had passed, and he'd obviously never recovered because she was here and he was right back in his feelings again. That pissed him off, which was why he was hesitant to go see her now.

Jess took a sip from her cup. "I know the history. I know that things didn't end well, but you don't know everything, El. There was more at play than she told you back then."

"It doesn't matter, Jess."

"It will when you know the truth."

El wanted to ask more, but knew Jess wouldn't share Avery's secrets with him.

"Listen, she needs you," Jess said. "More than

that, she wants you there. She won't say it, and gosh, I shouldn't have even told you what I did. I feel like it's a betrayal. But I'll do anything for her."

El's anger deflated at the look of desperation on Jess's face. "You know I won't say anything to her about this conversation, Jess."

"I know you won't."

"But I am wondering why you're asking me to help her if you feel like it's a betrayal."

"Because if my guess is correct, there's still love there. You don't like seeing her like this any more than me."

He received a page at that point. Glancing down at the device, he frowned. "I have to go, Jess."

He stood, but she grabbed his wrist. "Think about what I've said. Please?"

El glanced down at Jess. There were a few people milling around the halls outside the family room they were in. It was shift change, and groups of employees were leaving as others were making their way to work.

"I'll think about it. There's a lot *you* don't know, Jess." Starting with the turmoil Avery's leaving had thrust him into.

El was no stranger to women trying to use him. He was a Jackson, after all. He'd been born with status because of his last name. Women had been drawn to him because of it. They'd been bold in their intentions, too, coming up with all types of schemes to trap him. In high school, one girl had tried to pin another man's baby on him. During his freshman year in college, he'd caught a woman stealing from him.

El wasn't like his older brother, Lawrence. From

childhood, he'd tried to look at people through a clear lens and not let his past experiences keep him from seeing the best in people. But one too many scams, too many disingenuous women had taken their toll and almost hardened his heart. Until that day in the Michigan Union.

Avery had been different. She hadn't cared about his last name or his wallet. Her parents had never traveled in his family's circles, and Avery hadn't been interested in community status or the Jacksons of Ann Arbor. And he'd let her in, let himself fall for her brown skin and topaz eyes. And when she'd left him to pursue her career...when she'd walked away without even giving him a chance to give her the ring he'd purchased—and the promise he'd wanted to give her—he was devastated. It had taken months to work through it. Did he really want to jump back in headfirst?

"Trust me when I say that I don't need to know," Jess said. "It doesn't matter anyway. There's one thing I've learned through my own situation and that's time is precious. We could be sitting here talking about Avery's funeral."

El clenched her hand, jarred by the feeling that assaulted him at Jess's words. "Avery" and "funeral" were two words that didn't belong together in a sentence. Just the thought of it made him sick to his stomach.

"Jess, don't do that."

"It's true." She stood. "It was a very real possibility and you know that. I've lost too much already, and I can't lose Avery. She means so much to me. I wouldn't be here if it wasn't for her. She saved my life, and I'm returning the favor. If that means I have to beg you to be present, I will."

El snickered. "You do realize that Avery has to want to fight. What makes you think I can do anything to help? As you said, there is history, water under the bridge. My presence could hurt her recovery."

He didn't really believe that. It was an excuse, just like so many he'd come up with over the last several hours. Essentially, Jess hadn't said anything that was untrue. Helping people cope *was* what he did for a living. Helping people adjust to health calamities like Avery's was what he'd built his practice on. So why was he so hesitant to give her, someone he cared for deeply, the care that he'd give a stranger? One reason was that being close to her, seeing her, was trouble for him. Trouble that he didn't want or need at that point in his life.

When his pager buzzed again, he smiled at Jess. "I have to get to the floor. We'll talk later, but think about what I said."

Chapter 5

"Good morning, Ms. Montgomery." Avery turned toward the voice of her home care nurse, Rosa.

Avery had been awake for hours, unable to sleep. She'd been released from the hospital, after spending several days there. Once her blood pressure had stabilized, she'd managed to convince her doctors that she was fine to go home. They'd granted her request, on the condition that she hire a private duty healthcare staff to take over care. Instead of returning to the hotel, even though she'd never technically checked out, she'd decided to go to her family home to recuperate. The reason was two-fold—it was more comfortable and private.

Although the thought of having a nurse come into her space was frustrating, it was better than top-of-the-hour visits from nurses wanting to check her vitals and doctors arriving at the crack of dawn for rounds. One thing was certain, the hospital was not for the weak of heart, and Avery was grateful to be in the warmth of her childhood home. With only a few people allowed to visit aside from Jess, Rosa and the Personal Support Assistant she'd hired, it had been quiet.

"Morning, Rosa," she grumbled.

Rosa had been introduced to her when she was discharged two days ago and was a lovely person, patient and kind. Avery sensed she was in her mid-to-late fifties but wouldn't dare ask. Her mother once told her never to ask a lady her age, and that tip had stuck with her.

"It's a beautiful day," Rosa announced before placing cool fingers against the radial artery on Avery's wrist to take a pulse. "I can take you for a walk if you'd like."

Avery didn't want to go for a walk, because the thought of being outside worried her. There were many reasons to stay indoors, one being her high profile. She didn't want to take the chance of anyone spotting her taking a stroll, or someone snapping pictures of her and selling them to the highest bidder for a baseless story in the blogs or on social media.

Although she wasn't a vain person or overly concerned about her looks, she didn't want to be the next "hot mess" headline. Despite her celebrity status, Avery had tried to stay out of the spotlight. Normally, she was incognito enough to avoid reporters. Yet, the last several months, she'd been in and out of the gossip magazines because of a few explosive cast changes and a purported link between herself and one of the male cast members.

The alleged relationship between her and Blair Wallace had blown up because one of the paparazzi snapped a pic of her and him at a restaurant. The meal had been innocent, but that didn't stop the hashtags, Instagram commentary and gossip about "BlaiVery."

If word got out about her illness, she had no doubt Ann Arbor would be a prime destination for paparazzi.

"I don't want to go outside, Rosa." Avery sighed heavily. "I'm fine here."

Avery had told herself that she would at least try to get some work done once she was released from the hospital. So far, though, she hadn't been motivated to do anything but listen to the news.

"Your vitals look good," Rosa continued. "Have you had any improvements with your vision?"

Since she'd regained consciousness in the hospital, Avery had prayed, pleaded, bargained with God to restore her vision. To no avail. "No," she answered.

"I'm sorry, hun."

Avery heard Rosa scribbling on something. Writing. Like Avery needed to be doing at that very moment. The network had called numerous times, according to Jess. Her friend had stalled for time at Avery's request. But soon they'd grow impatient. What would she do then?

"Did you need anything?" the nurse asked. "I can bring you some breakfast. I wasn't sure what you had in your refrigerator, so I brought several things from the hospital to eat."

Food was the last thing Avery wanted, but that

wasn't what the nurse wanted to hear, so she told her, "Maybe in a little while. Thank you."

"Try to get some rest," Rosa told her. "I'll be right downstairs if you need anything."

Avery wanted to roll her eyes and scream that she couldn't rest. Not when she couldn't figure out her life. Not when she felt so damn vulnerable behind the veil of darkness that had become her world. Instead, though, she said, "I'll try."

When she heard the door close, she squeezed her eyes shut, then opened them again, stupidly hoping something would have changed. Nothing. Using her fingertips, she patted the bed for the television remote control Jess had left with her and pushed the Power button. The sound of the television filled the room, and she recognized the voice of one of Detroit's popular news anchors.

She listened as the woman went over the local news before she was joined by the weatherman. Partly sunny, high of seventy-eight degrees. One of those perfect spring days that she used to love as a kid.

There was something about springtime that usually gave her new hope. But instead of feeling that same hope that had gotten her through many tough moments, she felt nothing. Would she always feel that way?

Avery wasn't dumb. She knew it wasn't the end of the world. Many people were blind and lived fulfilling lives. They enjoyed movies, walks in the park, Broadway shows and reading. Technology was such that she could buy a gadget that identified the colors of the clothes in her closets. She didn't have to drive. Hell, she barely drove now. She enjoyed having a driver take her where she needed to go. It wasn't like she couldn't still travel or speak to large crowds. But damn...what would happen to her career?

There were people who would chew her up and spit her out if they found out about her illness, her vulnerability. Some of those people were supposedly on her team. Avery knew it was coming, someone was going to find out that she was blind and try to steal her life, take over the show she'd created.

Briefly she'd considered asking Luke to return early from his vacation, but ultimately decided against it. He'd worked hard and deserved the time off. Jess had stepped in in his absence, and promised to do her best to make sure no one found out the extent of Avery's illness. But Jess couldn't control the craziness of sneaky paparazzi.

Avery was a realist. It was highly unlikely they could keep her condition under wraps for an extended period of time, or even her location. For a few more days, maybe, but not any longer than that. When she'd left the hospital, they'd snuck her out and used a decoy "Avery" to go back to the hotel to throw off lingering reporters.

It was up to Avery to get through this and still be who she was. As frightening as it was, she had to find a way to move forward. And hope that God heard her prayers. In the meantime, her agent Walter had arranged a press release that gave little information on the extent of her sickness, but would appease the masses for a while.

Rosa called up to her from downstairs to announce that she had a visitor—a Dr. Jackson. Avery gave the okay to send him up. Drake had already called and told her he would be by to see her.

"Hey."

It was El, though. Avery closed her eyes and let the low timbre of El's voice sweep through her body. *He came.* "Hi."

The sound of a chair scraping against the floor drew her attention toward her right. "How are you?"

He was closer now, most likely sitting next to the bed. "How do you think?" She didn't mean it to come out so bitchy. "I'm sorry. I'm just frustrated."

"It's okay." He chuckled. "You're allowed. I figured it was time I come by and check on you. Where's Jess?"

Avery had insisted her friend go back to work, at least for a few hours a day. With Rosa there with her, and her parents returning from their trip soon, Avery wanted her friend to get back to her life. Once Jess had left that morning for her first day back to work, though, Avery had immediately regretted it. Yes, the home healthcare staff was there and her security was posted in her parents' living room, but it wasn't the same. The loss of someone friendly and familiar near her made her feel alone and lonely, as cliché as it sounded.

After she filled him in on Jess's whereabouts, she said, "I wasn't sure you'd come over to see me."

"What can I say? I couldn't stay away."

El's confession made her senses sing. "Thank you. I'm sorry." The apology was long overdue, but she needed to say it. "You didn't deserve the way I treated you when you were just trying to help me."

She felt the warmth of his palm over her hand. "No need to apologize for that, Avery. It's okay."

Avery nodded, twisted her finger in her sheet. "El, I feel myself falling down a bottomless pit of pain and anxiety. If I could just…" She let out a long sigh, then shrugged. "It doesn't matter anyway."

"It does matter how you feel."

She snorted. "Are you saying that as El, the psychiatrist?" Avery wasn't sure how he was supposed to answer that question. What else would he be to her? It wasn't like they were friends. Which is precisely the reason visiting Ann Arbor was so hard for her. Being near him, even for one second, had her galloping full speed ahead with visions of them rekindling at least a friendship.

Avery wanted to tell him the truth, confess to him the real reason she'd walked away from him.

El squeezed her hand. "I'm saying that because it's true. How you feel matters."

"How do you do that?"

"Do what?"

"Act like everything is okay all the time. Even though you and I both know it's not."

"Occupational hazard," he said with a laugh. "Let's go."

Surprised, Avery frowned. "What? Where are we going?"

"For a walk."

"I don't think that is a good idea, El. I don't want anyone to know I'm blind."

"The hospital has not disclosed any details on your condition to the media, Avie. You know that. No one knows anything at this point. And there weren't any suspicious people milling in the neighborhood when got here."

Avery warmed at the fact that he'd called her by her nickname. He was the only one who'd ever called her Avie. It was his thing, and she'd always felt safe when he'd said it. Today was no exception.

Swallowing past a lump that had formed in her throat, she croaked, "Yeah, but… You said it yourself—at this point, I don't expect my whereabouts to remain a secret much longer. Besides, I must look crazy right now. I just don't want to give the gossips anything to talk about. I'm glad that you came to see me, but—"

"Avie, stop."

Avery clamped her mouth shut. She let her head drift toward his voice. "Please," she managed to say. "Don't make me go outside. I'm…"

Her voice sounded foreign, even to her own ears. The word "scared" was on the tip of her tongue, but she didn't want to give it any power to take over her life.

His hand on her arm soothed her fraying nerves. His touch was almost healing, and she wanted to snuggle against him, wrap herself up in him.

"I'm walking with you." He squeezed her arm, and helped her out of the bed. "Do you really think I'd let anything happen to you?"

Avery found herself shaking her head. "No," she whispered.

"Then let's go."

El led Avery down the stairs, and let Rosa and the security guard know that he was taking Avery out for much needed fresh air.

Several minutes later, Avery was standing outside with El, arm in arm. She pushed a strand of hair behind her ear, and her fingertips brushed the glasses El had placed on her face before they walked out of the room. It felt strange to be out of the bed. Of course, she'd walked around the house with assistance, but this was different. She was actually outside, getting ready to walk through the neighborhood that had made her a household name.

It was one of the more mature neighborhoods in the Ann Arbor, and there was a mixed population of people from different nationalities, races and cultures. There was a huge, active neighborhood association, but each street also had its own association. Community block parties and picnics were common occurrences growing up. Every year, they had a Fourth of July Extravaganza, a Halloween Prank Contest and a Battle of the Christmas Lights. And like every neighborhood, there was a fair share of drama, which had sparked her idea to write about her neighbors, their kids and their kids' kids.

"Where are we going?" she murmured.

"I told you, for a walk. What I want you to do is just concentrate on the noise you hear. Try picking out specific sounds as we walk. Don't worry about falling. I've got you."

Relaxing a little, she tried to let go of the thoughts swarming her mind. "I'm nervous."

"Don't be. It's going to be okay."

She tried to do as he'd instructed, listen to the things around her, but she found it hard to concentrate on anything. She wondered who was in their yard working or riding a bike through the neighborhood, if anyone would approach her. And she thought about the cologne El was wearing that day. He smelled delicious, like pears and wood. It wasn't strong, but it definitely evoked feeling in her.

"We're going to step onto the porch," he said.

Stepping forward, she immediately registered the hard cement under her feet. It was cool against the soles of her ballerina flats. He turned her and she heard him greet someone before he led her forward.

When a loud horn blared, she jumped. "It's okay," he murmured. "I've got you."

"You better," she muttered with a soft giggle. "Don't let me fall."

He chuckled. "Never."

The sound of a lawnmower in the distance reached her ears. As they walked, El whispered things to her about their surroundings, things that she remembered from the last time she'd been to her parents' neighborhood for the family funeral months ago.

"Doesn't sound like much has changed," she told him.

"Not really. They are building an organic food grocery store around the corner, though."

"Mom told me about that. I'll have to make sure I incorporate some of these changes into the show."

"Yeah, get right on that."

Avery noticed the tension in his voice when she mentioned her show. She wanted to ask him about it, but thought better of it, preferring to keep the conversation positive.

As they moved down the street in silence, she thought about the times he'd come to her house to visit during breaks. They'd spent many days and nights there together when they were dating, talking and hanging out at the neighborhood park.

El was three years older and had a wealth of experience compared to her. She'd been a sheltered daughter of older parents. Before she'd enrolled at the university, she'd rarely spent the night away from her parents. Except when she'd visited Jess, and even that wasn't much. She'd always preferred Jess to come to her house. Jess preferred it that way, as well, because her mother worked a lot and she hated being in their apartment alone.

Avery heard a piano playing and grinned. Mr. Maddox was still at it. One of her neighbors was a jazz musician and woke up every morning to practice his piano with the windows wide open. She remembered lying out on the grass while he gave mini-concerts on warm summer nights.

The neighborhood was pretty self-sufficient, as well. When she was growing up, there had been a community garden, a pool and even a corner store owned by Old Man Johnson. It had been a sad day when he died. He'd been like a great-uncle to the neighborhood kids. Everyone was devastated when a heart attack took him away from them.

"Is the haunted house on the corner still there?" she asked. "Mom told me someone had expressed interest in buying it."

"It is," El told her. "Still there and still as ugly as it ever was."

The haunted house she was referring to once belonged to the Connor family. Rumor had it that Mr. Connor had committed a heinous crime and buried bodies in the yard. For years, it was the only house in the neighborhood that was unkempt. Her parents had complained to the neighborhood association and even the city, but nothing was ever done. Avery remembered Halloweens when she and her friends scared themselves with stories about ghosts and murder in the Connor house while camping out in her backyard.

Avery felt a soft breeze in her face and she sighed. It felt good to be outside, and she was glad El had made her get off her ass and take a walk. The smell of grass and wind and flowers soothed her spirit, and for the first time, she realized she wasn't obsessing over the loss of her sight or what her next steps would be.

Before she knew it, she was smiling. She heard the sound of a basketball hitting pavement. Taking in a deep breath, she sighed. "We're at the park," she said.

"Yes," he told her.

After a few more steps he directed her to take a seat. Once she felt the hard wood against her behind she slumped back. The water from the fountain her father had donated was like music to her ears. An overwhelming peace enveloped her as she breathed in the air.

"Thank you," she whispered.

"For what?"

Avery felt El next to her, his shoulder touching hers. She felt the urge to lean into him, so she did. "For bringing me here."

"It's a special place."

The Congress Neighborhood Park had been commissioned by the neighborhood association, a group founded by her mother years ago. The goal was to provide a safe place for the residents and their children. There was a basketball court, a kickball field and a pavilion available for gatherings. The fountain was on the south side of the park, nestled between a gazebo and the community garden. Even now, after she'd traveled to some of the greatest landmarks in the world, the park topped her list of favorite places. She had often stolen away to the park to study or write. It was also there that El had told her he loved her the first time.

"That it is," she agreed. "I'm glad you brought me here."

"Avery, I..."

So, I'm back to Avery again. She tried to steel herself for what was going to come next. "Just say it, El. Is this about my sight? Did the doctors tell you anything? Is that why you're really here?"

Of course she knew the doctors shouldn't disclose her personal health information to El, but she also knew how it worked there. He was one of their own and she figured there were plenty of staff who would tell him what he wanted to know.

"No. Your doctors haven't told me anything. Listen," She felt him shift and then felt the hard point of his knee against hers. He picked up her hand. "I know you know the medicine involved, the prognosis for someone with your symptoms."

"I know." Her shoulders fell.

"But you also know the power of negativity, and how important it is to be positive. You can still get your sight back. In the meantime, though, you have to try to find ways of dealing with the loss of your vision. You can do that by honing in on your other senses, appreciating things like the morning air, the smell of coffee in the morning, the sound of the trees swaying in the wind. Those are things you can tap into when you're feeling anxious."

"I hear you, but I keep wondering...why me?"

"Stress. More and more younger people—women—are having strokes, Avery. And it's because of stress. You're doing too much, not taking care of yourself. I bet you don't sleep or eat like you should."

Avery let out a humorless chuckle. "You do know me well." Truth was, Avery rarely slept. Most nights, she was up writing until the wee hours of the morning. She was lucky if she got four hours of sleep every night. Luke already had to slip food in her laptop bag, or send her food to the studio.

His fingertips brushed her cheek and he turned her head. "Your life isn't over."

"This is hard. I've tried to think this through, to come up with a plan. But mostly I feel empty. Like someone took a knife and hollowed me out like a pumpkin." She let her head fall back so the sun could warm her face.

Avery had been through some crazy shit in her life. She had to admit that a lot of that stuff occurred after she'd left Michigan and El. But she'd managed to survive, to make it, even if it was by a thin string. But this...

"Avie, you're still you. Still smart, still driven, still beautiful."

"El." Tears filled her eyes as his finger brushed over her lips. "I don't feel..."

When she felt his breath against her lips, smelled the faint scent of coffee on it, she couldn't finish her sentence, let alone gather her thoughts. What had she been going to say again?

"Avie, you *are* beautiful."

That's it. That was what she was going to say, that

she didn't feel beautiful. El used to be able to finish her sentences. She guessed he still had that talent because he'd seemingly read her mind.

Her lips parted and she leaned closer. When she felt his hand cradle her face, her eyes fluttered closed. *Oh, my.* Holding his wrists to keep his hands in place, she sucked in a deep breath, anticipated his next move.

"You're here, what? A week, and I can't think about anything else," he said against her mouth.

Avery felt his tongue streak across her bottom lip and dug her fingernails into his skin. "I know the feeling."

And she did. Except it had felt like that every day, even before she'd stepped foot in Ann Arbor. There was no rhyme or reason. It just was. He was in her heart, running through her mind constantly. It was almost like he haunted her. And she was okay with it because it had been her only connection to him for years.

"You do?" His lips brushed over the corners of her mouth, and she groaned.

"Yes," she admitted, the word sounding more like a breathy sigh.

"Avie?"

Her name on his lips made her heart quiver with desire. "Hmm?"

Then, his mouth was over hers. In that moment, she didn't care where she was. She didn't even care that she couldn't see him. Just the feel of his lips against hers, the lure of his breath mingling with hers was enough. She relaxed into him, reveling in him.

El had always been a good kisser. A phenomenal

one, in fact. A kiss was never just mouth to mouth, tongue to tongue. A kiss from El had always been a full body event.

And this… *Damn.* This was no exception. It wasn't a *feel better* kiss. It wasn't even a *feel sorry* kiss. It was the type of kiss she wrote about, waxed poetic about in her scripts. He kissed her like his very salvation was dependent on her lips. El sucked on her bottom lip before trailing a line of kisses over her jawbone and then back up to her mouth. He nipped at her, slid his tongue against hers until her limbs felt weak.

"Avie," he murmured against her neck.

His hands felt so good against her body, his fingers feather soft against her arms, her neck, her face. He pulled her to him, taking her mouth in his again, drawing a low, almost guttural moan from her throat.

The sound of laughter coming from behind her broke through the haze of desire that had gripped her, and the warmth she'd felt only seconds earlier was replaced by the cold breeze against her flaming skin. Immediately she hugged herself, willing her heart to stop beating so fast and so hard.

El spoke to the person who'd interrupted a moment that she could only describe as nirvana. For those few glorious minutes, she'd felt happy.

"Let's go," he said, once again jarring her from her thoughts. "I better get you back."

Disappointed, she simply nodded and allowed him to escort her back to her parents' house.

Chapter 6

What the hell was I thinking?

It had been a few days since he'd kissed Avery silly in the park. And El had asked himself that same question several times since then. There were no answers, though. He made a living helping people figure things out. But for the life of him, he couldn't figure out why he'd opened that door. A door that he'd thought was firmly shut a long time ago.

It frustrated him that he hadn't been able to control himself. Being with her, sitting on the same bench where he'd confessed his love all those years ago had gotten to him. And to see her reaction to being there, the way she smiled and breathed in *their* space, did things to him, propelled him forward.

Her mouth. Yes, that's what it was. He'd missed her mouth, those full lips. He'd even missed the tiny mole on her upper lip, the one she hated and tried to hide all the time.

Obviously, he'd underestimated the power she held over him. El didn't want to obsess over her smile, those eyes that had always been windows to her soul. Yet he'd found himself lying awake at night, tormented by visions of her, dreaming of kissing her until she begged him to... *Shit.*

El rubbed his head, frustration rolling off him in waves. He didn't want to want her. Hell, he didn't want to feel anything for her. But he did, and that made him angry.

Avery had always fascinated him, made him feel things that seemed to overtake his common sense. And he'd certainly lost all sense when he'd pulled her into that kiss.

After a second night of tossing and turning, El found himself at work in the emergency room. He'd tried everything he could think of to go to sleep, including reading a romance novel. Nothing worked. And it was his own fault. He was the one who'd messed up, who'd disrupted his own sleep pattern with his antics. Because he'd kissed her. Then he'd walked her back into her parents' house and left without another word.

It was a quiet night in the ER, but El had a steady flow of patients. Since Drake was also at work, during a break, they headed to the cafeteria for coffee.

"You doing alright?" Drake asked after he took a sip of his black coffee. "You seem distracted, which is not like you."

El shrugged. "I'm fine."

Drake eyed him as if he knew he was lying, but didn't call him on it. "Have you seen Avery?"

Every part of him wanted to talk to Drake about the Avery situation. But he wasn't sure it was wise to say anything aloud. Drake didn't need to know that El had kissed Avery.

For all intents and purposes, Avery wasn't his responsibility anymore. They'd broken up a long time ago. She shouldn't be clouding his mind, gripping his heart with her fist. Hell, he'd counseled patients on knowing when to let go of old relationships, so he should know better.

He didn't.

"I went to see her today," Drake continued. "Left her about an hour ago."

"How is she? Has she had any improvement?"

El didn't know why he'd even asked. He knew how she was. He'd checked in on her progress with her doctors and Jess. He just couldn't bring himself to go see her again. *Not after I kissed the hell out of her.*

Drake shook his head. "Not really. Her blood pressure has remained stable since she was released, but her sight still hasn't returned."

El knew that didn't bode well for her long-term prognosis, and he couldn't face her because of it. *And that kiss.* He was a coward, plain and simple. He knew beyond a shadow of a doubt that he wouldn't be able to take that look in her eyes, the look of despair he was sure would be shining in her jewel-toned orbs when he saw her. Especially after he'd implored her to be positive.

"According to Jess, she hasn't really slept, though.

Yesterday, she broke her toe when she attempted to go to the bathroom without assistance."

Guilt welled up in El. Was he the reason she couldn't sleep?

"She had been working a little, though," Drake added. "On her foundation. Then she had a setback today."

"Is Jess still staying with her?" El asked.

Drake nodded. "You know she is. Apparently, her parents return from their trip today, which is good. She could use the extra support."

El nodded. Avery's parents would have been right by her side if they were in town. He knew there had to be a good reason they weren't. "And her sisters?"

"Jess didn't say." Drake frowned. "I'm guessing they're still at odds."

Avery hadn't spoken with her sisters in years. It had a lot to do with how they'd treated her all of her life. They'd never even tried to have a relationship with Avery, and had pretty much acted like she didn't exist.

"El, I'm not trying to start something, but…"

"I kissed her," El blurted out. "That's why I haven't been back to see her."

Drake's eyes widened. "You kissed her? When?"

El told Drake the entire story, starting from his visit to their walk to the kiss and finally to how he'd walked away and didn't go back.

"That was a jerk move," Drake said.

El couldn't argue with that. Not only was he a self-ish jerk, he was an asshole. "You're right, I messed up by kissing her. Then, I purposely stayed away because I'm having a hard time dealing with my actions that day in the park.

"After everything, I don't know why I did it. But the mere fact that I did is making me feel uncomfortable. I don't want to hand Avery any more power over me than she already has."

"So you're running?"

"I wouldn't call it that." *Out loud.* Smiling at a passing nurse, El started toward his office.

"Come on, man." Drake fell in beside him. "You're not this guy."

El stopped in his tracks. Turning to his nephew, he took a deep breath. "What, Drake? What the hell do you need me to say?"

"How about get your head out of your ass, stop feeling sorry for yourself and go get your woman." Drake sighed heavily. "El, she needs you." He met El's eyes again. "And real talk? You need her, too."

Sighing, El eyed Drake. His nephew was absolutely correct. After everything, he needed Avery. The mass of his conflicting emotions about her was driving him insane. Obviously, he wanted her just as fiercely as he ever had. All it took was one look into her eyes, and he wanted to do whatever it took to have her. He wanted her to choose him—over her career, over everything and everyone else.

It was sobering for him to acknowledge the fact that, despite everything, he would choose her in a heartbeat if she let him. That, coupled with the resentment that still spread in his gut when he saw her, made him feel crazy.

El sighed. "So, what happened today?"

"She saw her nurse's shadow today," Drake explained.

Frowning, El said, "That's a good thing."

"Except it lasted for all of two seconds. She flipped out and canceled her appointment with the occupational therapist."

"I'll go see her," El told Drake.

Drake nodded. "I think it's best."

El grimaced when Drake squeezed his shoulder. "Get your hands off me."

Drake laughed. "I feel like the older brother today. You should give me a dollar for this session."

When Drake had been going through his own romance woes with Love, he would often come to El's office and plop a dollar bill down on his desk for "doctor–patient confidentiality."

El snorted. "Wait for it."

They talked for a few more minutes before El excused himself to check on a patient.

An hour later, El was standing in the doorway of Avery's room at her parents' house. She was sitting up in bed, her eyes open and forward. Her foot was propped up on a pillow, her swollen toe visible even from where he was standing. He'd asked Rosa to give them a few moments, to which the older woman happily agreed.

"Are you just going to stand there watching me?" Avery asked softly.

El wasn't surprised she knew he was there. If anything, he'd expected it. She'd always sensed when he was near, just like he knew when she was around. Some religious folks would call it a *soul tie*.

Lawrence had rarely gone to church. He did so only when there was a program or he was being honored with a community award or making a huge donation for appearances. But while living in Las Vegas, El had made friends with a kid whose father was a pastor at a local church. As a result, he'd visited the small congregation on many Sundays and had even attended Sunday school on countless occasions.

His Sunday school teacher, Sister Mildred, used to sneak him peppermints every time he was there. It was the highlight of his week. One particular Sunday, he remembered arriving early just to talk to Sister Mildred. She was a petite woman with wide hips and a crooked smile. But she was one of the best people he knew. Her hugs were like warm cocoons, and that day he'd needed one.

El remembered walking into the small church and getting Sister Mildred's attention right away. She left her class for him that day, walked with him to the corner and let him vent to her about Lawrence and his parents and how alone in the world he'd felt. Instead of giving him what he'd come for—a hug— she'd pointed at him and told him that he had to stop letting his brother and his parents steal his joy.

That one day, those few words had changed his life. And looking at Avery, so vulnerable, so alone, made him want to give her those same words. But he sensed they would ring hollow to her. He couldn't imagine being in her shoes. He couldn't fathom not being able to see. So the only thing he could do was help her *see* life through her ears, her mouth, her fingers.

Stepping into the room, he said, "Not anymore."

Avery crossed her arms in front of her chest, her mouth set into a hard line, but she remained silent.

El had expected her wrath. He did kiss her and disappear. But he hadn't expected her silence. "No smart comment, no kicking me out of your room?"

Avery frowned, but didn't speak.

He touched her toe lightly, cringing when she flinched. "I'm sorry about your toe."

She closed her eyes hard before sighing. Then her topaz orbs were open and on him. Tilting his head, he wondered what she saw, if anything. "You kissed me," she bit out. "Then you left."

"I know, and I'm sorry. I was wrong for leaving you the way I did, for not coming back until now."

Her shoulders sagged, but her jaw was still tight. "I don't need your apology."

"Too bad, because you got it. And I'm not taking it back. Whether you forgive me is up to you."

She lifted her chin. "Why did you come?"

"I couldn't not come. I picked up some lunch. Figured we could go outside on the deck and eat."

Avery blinked and her mouth fell open before she clamped it shut. "Why?"

He chuckled at the surprised look on her face. "Because I wanted to. Is there a problem?"

"You left, El," she repeated, this time without the ire. "I figured you didn't want to be bothered with me. So…"

"I just apologized and I'm here now. So…"

She rolled her eyes, and he couldn't help it. He laughed. When they were dating, she'd hated when he mimicked her that way.

"Listen." He brushed his fingers over her ankle.

"We've had years to move past this, and neither of us has. That's a conversation for another day, though. Today, I just want to eat Italian food and chill out with you. I know you're hurting, and I just want to help you. Let me."

Her chin trembled, which had always proved to be his undoing. "Not if you're going to kiss me again and then leave. I can't take it."

That was the Avery he knew. Direct. "I promise I won't kiss you and leave. Does this mean that you want me to kiss you and stay?"

His attempt at humor was probably too much for the time and place, but she finally laughed. "I just want to feel better," she said.

"Well, let's work on that." He helped her to her feet, holding her so that she wasn't putting her weight on her injured foot. "But before we go, I have one thing to say."

Resisting the urge to pull her closer and kiss her, he stepped back. El wondered if that feeling would ever go away.

"What?" she asked.

"I'm not trying to be funny, but you need to put a comb in that hair," he whispered. "And shave those legs."

She giggled. "I hate you."

"Seriously? Stop being stubborn and get rid of that hot mess of a bun on your head."

Chapter 7

Avery felt peace for the first time since her stroke. And she knew, beyond a shadow of a doubt, that it was because of El. Despite everything she'd done to ruin their friendship, their relationship, he'd still come to her aid. He'd made her laugh. *Even though he made fun of my hair.*

"Have a seat," El ordered softly.

Avery felt behind her and gingerly sat down on the toilet. "El?"

"Shh. Don't ask any questions."

She wasn't sure what El had in mind. He'd given Rosa the rest of the afternoon off, telling the nurse that he was taking care of Avery. Next, he'd called Jess and told her there was no need to stop by the house before she headed to the airport to pick up Phil and Jan.

Finally, El had led her to the bathroom, promising to help her get herself together. He'd run the shower for her and stood on the other side of the curtain while she washed.

Once she was done, he'd handed her a towel and helped her out of the shower. Now she was sitting in her parents' bathroom, wrapped in a towel, waiting for his next move.

A moment later, she felt his fingers travel up her calf, over her knees, before his hands rested on her hips. Gasping, she gripped the arms of the chair he'd pulled into the bathroom and bit down on her bottom lip.

In the background, she heard the water of the sink running. She opened her mouth to ask what he was getting ready to do, but clamped it shut when a hint of lavender wafted to her nose as he applied her cool shaving gel to her legs.

"Oh, God," she mumbled.

His low chuckle seeped into her skin, straight to her core and she fought the urge to moan. She held on to the chair for dear life as he slowly shaved her legs.

By the time he was finished, her skin felt like it was on fire, and she welcomed the feeling. It had been so long since Avery had been touched by a man so intimately. Three years, to be exact. But it felt good; she felt alive under his gentle caress.

In that moment, Avery wished she could see El, read his thoughts in his eyes. She wondered if he was as affected as she.

"El?" she managed to say, albeit on a shaky breath.

"Avie." He leaned into her, his forehead resting on her bosom. She resisted the urge to wrap her arms and her legs around him. The last thing she needed was the rejection of him pushing her away.

So she waited. Until she couldn't take it anymore. He was too close, too quiet. And she was breathing hard and loud. She gripped his shoulders. "El?" she called again.

"Let's get you dressed. You need to eat."

The warmth of his body disappeared when he stood, and she wanted to cry out in protest. But when he grabbed her hand, she took it and let him help her to her feet.

Avery dressed quickly in the yoga pants and T-shirt that El had picked out for her. Soon she was seated beside him outside on the deck, enjoying the light spring breeze He'd brought lasagna, salad and breadsticks from her favorite local Italian restaurant.

While they ate, Avery imagined El's face. Eyes that she had lost herself in more times than she could count. They were warm pools of milk chocolate and, in that moment, she wished more than anything that she could see them, swim in the heat of his gaze.

But the smell of him, the warmth of his body next to hers, was doing something to her. His presence had rained that sweet peace down on her, and she wanted to hold on to it for as long as she could.

"Do you still have the convertible?" she asked.

"No," he answered softly. "Got rid of it when you left."

Sucking in a deep breath, she prayed his admission wouldn't zap away the inner peace she'd felt a few seconds ago. Avery knew she'd hurt El, but he wasn't the only one she'd hurt.

For a while after she'd left, it felt like she'd ripped

her own heart out of her chest. She'd picked up the phone several times to call him, to beg him to take her back. Avery had written letters, composed emails...but could never bring herself to send them.

The truth was ugly. They'd become so close, so fast. Yet, in the end, she'd let it go. It was her biggest regret. Not only that she'd left, but that she'd let someone get into her head enough to make her doubt her worth.

There was no secret that Avery's family wasn't rich. They weren't poor, but they couldn't afford to send her to college. Her father was older, retired. Both of her parents had been on a fixed income at the time. Avery had worked hard in school to earn as much scholarship money as she could.

Despite being from the same town, she didn't know any member of his family before meeting El. It wasn't like they lived in the same neighborhood, or even on the same side of town. Although her middle-class neighborhood was considered one of the nicest on the east side of Ann Arbor, it was nothing compared to the massive home of Dr. Law, as everyone called El's brother.

The Jacksons went to charity balls and galas while the Montgomery family's idea of fun was a movie or a trip to the Sleeping Bear Dunes above Lake Michigan or a picnic at Detroit's Belle Isle.

In all the years she and El were together, Dr. Law hadn't had much to say to her. It was as if she wasn't even a blip on his radar. It had never bothered her, though, because El didn't spend a lot of time with his older brother. The two were so different, like night and day. It amazed Avery that they were even related.

So when Dr. Law cornered her at the hospital one day during her fourth year of medical school, she was nervous, anxious. Turns out the slight anxiety was warranted. The older man had looked down on her, told her that it was time that she let El be the man he was groomed to be and let him go. Dr. Law had even gone so far as to offer to pay off her student debt if she left town and never returned.

The memory of that conversation still made Avery sick to her stomach. And Dr. Law hadn't stopped there. He'd basically told her she was beneath a man of El's pedigree, that she simply wasn't good enough to be a Jackson. Then he'd thrown in that El would never marry her, never consider her more than a bed warmer.

Avery closed her eyes and willed her mind not to go there. She was having a good day so far. She didn't need to travel that road again. But she'd already slid deep into those memories, including the way she'd felt, how belittled she'd been.

Even so, she'd had no intention of giving up on El just because Dr. Law said so. She'd even dug in her heels and refused to give that man the satisfaction. Unfortunately, that hadn't been the last time Dr. Law came to visit. Each visit left her feeling a little more unsure of her place in El's life. So when the book deal and subsequent television option happened, she'd accepted it and made her decision to leave. Still, she couldn't quite let El go, so they'd done the long-distance thing. But even miles away, Dr. Law's words had continued to haunt her and finally she'd given in and broke up with El.

"Where are you, Avie?" El asked, pulling her from her thoughts.

Could she tell him the truth, finally? Would it change anything? Swallowing, she grumbled, "Just thinking about life."

"What about life?"

Avery shrugged. "Thinking about my choices," she lied.

Since she'd arrived in town, she'd been thinking about how different life would have been had she stayed. But she'd also thought of how her choice to leave had led to something good. She now had the power and the money to help young girls who wanted to attend college but couldn't see a way in.

When she'd created *The Preserves*, she hadn't expected it to become the phenomenon it was; she hadn't expected the accolades, the offers, the opened doors. She hadn't even realized she wanted those things. She still wasn't sure if she did. But now that she was in this position, she wanted to do more, be better.

"Before I had the stroke, I had set a plan in motion to finally start a foundation. Since I've been home from the hospital, I've been working a little on that."

Avery had finalized the mission statement, hired a website designer and started compiling the list of potential donors. She'd even come up with a few ideas for the fund-raising event she wanted to have in the next month or so.

"Really?" El said. His voice sounded interested, but even that was El. "It's about time."

Avery smiled at his enthusiasm. She'd drilled her dream of creating a nonprofit into his head for

years. "When I was at the graduation, right before
the ceremony started, one of the student speakers introduced herself to me." Avery remembered the encounter fondly, the hope in the young woman's eyes,
the vision, the drive. "It was almost like looking into
a mirror when I saw the determination on her face to
be someone that changed the world."

"You've always had that determination, that fire."

She chuckled. "If I had more time, I would have
talked to her more, maybe invited her to come to
my house in Atlanta. I wanted to hear her story. My
original plan was to stay and talk to the students, but
my manager added a trip to LA at the last minute.
Therein lies the problem. The demands of my life,
the travel, the work…it doesn't really afford me time
to do the things I know I'm supposed to be doing.
Like paying it forward."

"Well, that's something you can change. Maybe
not right away, but with planning."

"I want to change it now. That's why I'd scheduled a vacation. After LA, I was supposed to come
back here and work on this foundation," Avery told
him. "Even now, knowing I can't see, I keep thinking this is still the perfect opportunity. Right? Now
I have even more time to devote to it. It's not like I
can travel for a while, or even write like I need to."

Avery's doctors had instructed her to avoid traveling by air for at least six weeks. That was good and
bad. Walter had done a good job of stalling the network executives who were still waiting to approve the
scripts. Planning extended time off was a risk, one
that she'd never even considered taking a week ago.
A week off, or even two, was one thing. But sitting

on the sidelines for six weeks felt like career suicide. In Hollywood, there was always someone waiting to take your spot. But now…she couldn't help but wonder if it was worth her health to continue driving on all cylinders.

"There will always be something that has the potential to come between you and your dreams," El said, once again breaking her train of thought. "You just have to seize the moment to effect change."

"I have so many obligations," she admitted softly.

"But you're sick, Avie. You had a stroke, you lost your vision. You need to unplug to heal. That's important. You can't be Avery Montgomery, show producer, writer, if you're dead."

Avery thought about El's comments. He was absolutely right. She'd run her body into the ground. It was time to make some changes. But…*how*?

"Question," El said.

"Go ahead."

"If you only had a few days to live, what would you want to do?"

"Honestly?" She wasn't sure if he was ready for her answer. The first thought that ran through her mind was him.

"Is there any other way?"

Avery heard the amusement in his voice and couldn't help the grin that formed as a result. El had made her promise a long time ago that they would always be honest with each other. Except she hadn't been honest about her reasons for breaking up with him. She wondered if there was anything he'd kept from her.

"Okay," she said. "I think I'd like to focus on my

legacy and spend as much time with my loved ones as I could."

Yep. That was the safe answer. The one least likely to get her in a whole lot of trouble.

"Well, that was pretty safe." El laughed. "Can you at least try not to give me the patented Avery Montgomery interview version?"

Sighing, she decided to go with the truth. "Fine. If I only had a few days to live, I'd want to spend it with you."

The silence that followed made her fidget in her seat. She couldn't see him or get a read on his reaction to her soft confession.

Is this going to be a repeat of the other day? Would El simply get up and leave, and disappear for another day or forever? Avery couldn't take back the words. They were the absolute truth. If El would just give her the roadmap back to his heart, she would happily travel it with no hesitation. It wouldn't matter how hard, how rough the terrain, if doing so would give her even one more minute, one more second with him.

Avery shook her head. It was those thoughts that made her feel unhinged, desperate where El was concerned. And that was not her. She was who she was in the industry for a reason. She didn't take any crap from people. She was strong, assertive, a long way from that woman who'd let Dr. Law get to her. It was a conundrum, of sorts. On the other hand, she was just Avery, the woman who was hopelessly in love with Dr. Elwood Jackson, the woman who'd let his brother get in her head and run her away from the love of her life.

"You asked for the truth," she muttered. "I gave it to you."

"I better get this cleaned up," he said, not addressing her confession. Then, she heard him stand, and walk away, leaving her alone in the space of uncertainty once again.

El was pissed. More than that, he felt stuck. Stuck in his feelings for a woman who had essentially broken his heart. Loving Avery was easy. He'd never actually stopped. But there was the rub. Nothing had changed, including the reasons they weren't together anymore. Oh, and the pesky truth that they didn't even live in the same city.

Even if El thought he could trust her again, they had a physical distance barrier that would prevent him from trusting it. Especially since it hadn't worked before. At this stage in his career, he was happy where he was. El was a well-respected young black doctor at a top medical facility. He loved what he did for a living. It didn't feel like work to him, to help his patients, to be in the hospital day in and day out.

He glanced out the patio window at her seated on the deck. He'd hurt her by leaving without answering her. Would it be like this with them forever? Consumed by hurt feelings, unsaid words?

El had struggled all day with his feelings for her and his never-ending attraction to her. Shaving her legs, helping her dress had nearly killed him. He'd wanted to kiss her, wanted to do more than kiss her. Good sex wouldn't solve anything, though. In the morning, the past would still be between them, threatening to destroy the tentative trust they'd started to rebuild.

Yes, the attraction was still there, but he couldn't give into the pull. Not right now. It wasn't the right time to get into their feelings with each other. Her parents would be arriving shortly, possibly in a matter of minutes. He hadn't seen Phil and Jan in years. Because when Avery had left, she wasn't the only person he'd lost. He'd lost people he'd grown close to, people he'd loved like family.

Letting out a slow, cleansing breath, he slid the patio door open and stepped onto the deck. "Hey."

Avery turned toward him, her face impassive. *God, she's so beautiful.* He took her hand and pulled her to him before he could think better of it. "I heard what you said."

Avery gasped, dug her fingernails into his forearm. "You didn't—"

"Now is not the time to discuss this. And I do want to talk about it. But you have a lot of work ahead of you. Let's get through that first. We can deal with 'us' later."

"Okay," she whispered.

"For now, let's take the long way back into the house." He led her down the deck stairs. Along the way, he described details of the house to her. The shutters were the same white they'd been when they were dating. He assumed she'd hired help to maintain the yard, so the grass was freshly cut. "Smell the grass?" he asked. "Looks like it was cut this morning. And the flowers are blooming."

She smiled and it was the loveliest sight he'd ever seen. "What kind of flowers?"

Swallowing, El described the daisies and purple lilacs on the bush in front of the garage. He also described the evidence of more to come. Janice Montgomery was a master gardener. When he was dating Avery, he'd spent a lot of time with her parents at their home.

When he'd visited, they would often be in the garden. Her father, Phil, could be seen cutting the grass or trimming the hedges and her mother would often be elbow deep in the dirt, planting flowers or pulling weeds.

He snapped a stem from the lilac bush and waved it under her nose. Avery moaned. "Oh, El. It smells divine."

"It does," he agreed. "I'm glad your parents kept the house."

"My parents didn't want to let it go, and neither did I. We had a lot of good times here. They don't spend a lot of time in Michigan, but it's here for them when they return for visits. It's theirs free and clear now, and I make sure it's taken care of in their absence." She squinted up at him.

Avery was worth a lot of money at this point in her career. She could buy her parents any house they wanted, but the fact that she maintained her childhood home from hundreds of miles away for her parents told him that there were still parts of the Avery he knew in her.

Frowning, he asked, "Are you registering the light of the sun?"

She nodded. "I can see light." Then she smiled again. "I can see light." The tears that shimmered in her eyes made his heart swell.

"Can you make out anything specific? Like color?"

"No, but it's not dark. That's a good sign. Isn't it?"

He grazed the back of his hand down her cheek before brushing his thumb under her eye, catching a tear. "It is definitely a good sign."

She grinned. "It's beautiful."

As he took in her face, her wide luminous eyes, he was hit with the compulsion to throw caution to the wind and take her in his arms. He wanted to kiss her until her knees buckled, drive away with her nestled against him.

As they neared the front door, he saw Jess's car pull into the driveway. A moment later, he heard Phil Montgomery say, "Avery, my baby girl! Hi, El!"

He turned to see the thin man standing next to the car, waving. The years had been good to Phil. He was tall and lean with light skin and light brown hair. Avery had shared her father's story with him years ago. Phil never knew his father, only that he was a white man who'd impregnated Phil's mother when she was very young. He'd also never known his mother, who'd died during childbirth. Phil was raised by his maternal aunt, which shaped the older man's view on life and love. It wasn't uncommon for Phil to be blunt in his observations, but El knew him to be a man of wisdom. His wit was unrivaled, and when he loved, he loved hard.

Smiling, El greeted the older man with a wave before leading Avery over to him. Phil promptly scooped her into his arms.

Avery cried as her father held her. He heard Phil whisper words of comfort, words of love to her while his hand rubbed soothing circles over her back. It wasn't the first time El had envied Avery's relationship with her parents. Early on, he'd realized that he'd give up all the money he had to have that type of relationship with a parent—or even his older brother.

When Phil set Avery on her feet again, he glanced up at El with identical topaz eyes. Grinning, Phil stepped forward and pulled El into a strong hug. Pulling back, with his hands on El's shoulders, Phil said, "I'm glad you're here. I appreciate you."

Letting out a breath he hadn't realized he was holding, El said, "I'm glad I'm here, too, Phil."

A loud scream sounded behind him as Janice Montgomery made her way over to them with Jess close behind her. Jan pulled Avery into a hug. Avery's mother was a petite woman with mocha skin and kind brown eyes. She'd worked her entire life as a nurse before retiring.

When Jan spotted El, she embraced him. El couldn't help but loosen up in her arms. Jan wasn't his mother, but she'd been a motherly figure to him. He'd missed her.

Several minutes and many more hugs later, they were inside the house. Jan had already brewed coffee.

"I plan to cook dinner tonight," Jan said, bringing over a tray with a coffee carafe and mugs.

El and Avery sat on the floral sofa in the living room. Jess sat on a smaller loveseat, and Phil made himself comfortable in his recliner.

"Coffee?" Jan asked El.

"Sure, Jan," he said, eyeing Avery. She'd grown silent, pensive, as soon as they'd stepped back inside the house. He wanted to ask her what was wrong, but refrained.

"Avery?" Jan called, a pained look in her eyes. "Do you want a cup of coffee, sweetie?"

Avery shook her head and gave a slight smile in the direction of her mother. "No, Mama. I'm fine."

Jan's eyes locked on El, and he wanted to reach out and give the older woman a hug. The devastation was plain on her face.

"Avery saw light today," El announced, not deterred by the thin, hard line that appeared on Avery's lips at his words. "That's a good sign."

Phil bowed his head and let out a slow breath, while Jan's gaze went up, looking at the ceiling. Relief. They were relieved at this news, which is why he'd mentioned it when he did.

"That's good," Phil finally said.

Jess nodded, tears welling in her eyes. "Avery, that's great."

Avery cleared her throat. "I guess. I'm back in the dark now. But at least there was light for a little while."

El placed his hand on her knee and didn't miss the way her parents and Jess followed his movement with their eyes. "It's a step in the right direction."

They sat for a while, chatting and drinking coffee. When Avery stood, explaining that she needed to excuse herself, Jess jumped to her feet and led her out of the room.

Once they were out of earshot, Jan asked, "El, how is she? She wouldn't really talk to us on the phone."

"She's doing a lot better than she was," El explained. "I finally got her to eat a full meal."

Phil nodded. "That's a good thing."

El knew from Jess that Avery had limited talk with

her parents while in the hospital because she wanted them to enjoy their vacation. Avery had waited to tell them about her stroke and subsequent blindness until they had docked in Seattle last night.

"I know this isn't your specialty, but in your professional opinion, do you think she'll regain her sight?" Jan asked him.

"Jan," Phil said. "You know more than most that there is no way to know that."

Phil rubbed his wife's back gently before pulling her into a tender hug. El turned away, affected by the scene before him.

Jess joined them after a few minutes. "Avery is tired. She wants to lie down." Jess's concerned gaze met his. "She said she's sorry."

El stared at the distraught expressions in Avery's parents' eyes and wanted to march upstairs and tell Avery to push through the emotions. Not just for them, but for herself. Instead, though, he stood. "I better get going, then."

"Before you go," Jess said. "Avery wants to see you."

Chapter 8

Avery sat on the edge of her bed. She felt guilty for making her parents sad. And even though she couldn't see them, she'd felt the tension in the room around her.

Yes, it was good to feel the warmth of their hugs and their presence, but things had taken a different turn once they were inside the house. It was a blow to go from the elation she'd felt at registering the light of the sun to being pitched back into a vat of darkness upon stepping into her childhood home.

She wanted to be okay for them, but she wasn't okay at that moment and felt it best that she excused herself for a bit. They'd taken care of her the best they knew how. She'd learned from them, grown with them and left them to find her own way before bringing them to live with her so she could take care of them. Avery considered it an honor to be able to give back to them what they'd given her. Security and love.

Now it felt like she was taking from them again and it frustrated her. They'd worked hard, done everything they were supposed to do. It was time for them to enjoy their life, not be thrust into the role of caregivers for her. Jess had told her that they all were happy to do whatever it took to help and support her, but Avery didn't feel right about it. Avery wanted to be able to take care of herself.

She sensed El near before she heard him. "You want to know how I knew you were in my room?"

"I already know," he said, his voice soft.

"I feel it. I always feel it. Even before I lost my sight, I could feel your presence like a warm blanket on a cold night. I need that. I need you to treat me like I'm normal. Treat me like I can see you."

"But you can't see me. You can't, Avie. What kind of person would I be if I acted like you could? I deal with patients every day that have lost something, whether it's their sight, their hearing, a loved one, their mind."

"I'm not one of your patients."

"No, you're not. You know, they need to be able to help you, Avery. It's not just for you. It's for them."

Avery closed her eyes at the low sound of El's voice. He wasn't mad, but he was firm. "I just need some time, okay?"

"You need all the support you can get. You're up here and they're down there with no clue on how to proceed."

"Did you ever stop to think how hard this is for me?"

"Oh, I know it's hard for you. I imagine it would be the same for me if I were in this position. But what are you going to do, Avie? Are you are going to stay in this room and in your head, or are you going to get your ass up and live your life?"

"I just need time, El," she snapped. "I need time to think. Which is why I called you up here."

"What is it? Do you want me to not come around for a few days?"

The bite in his tone made her flinch. Frowning, she said, "No. I called you up here to ask you to take me away from here."

Silence.

Avery had made her choice when Jess brought her up to the room. Avery loved her parents so much, but the only peace she felt was when she was with El. She needed that if she was going to get better.

"I've made a lot of mistakes," she continued. "I'm far from perfect. I'm stubborn. I don't really have a filter. I'm driven. I messed up. I broke us. I understand why you would hate me. I walked out on you after I promised I never would."

"I don't hate you, Avie. I could never hate someone I loved so much."

She didn't miss the "ed" at the end of the word that was running through her mind every second of the day when it came to him. "But you're angry and torn. And I get it. I deserve it. Like I said, I messed up. But I'm not afraid to tell you that I need you. I need you to stay with me. I need to stay with you. Take me away. Please."

The sound of his footsteps on the carpet drew her attention down. She closed her eyes and braced herself for the rejection. Why did she continually put herself in the position for him to reject her? He'd done it after he'd kissed her; he'd done it on the deck. What had made her think this time would be different, she didn't know.

The answer was easy, though. She loved him. She'd never stopped. And she wanted to be with him, be near him. Even if it was only temporary.

The air around her grew thick as she waited for his response. She felt the tips of his fingers across her cheek. "Avie." His voice warmed her insides like her favorite hazelnut coffee.

He pulled her to her feet. The soft scent of his cologne wafted to her nose and she shivered. "What?"

El leaned his forehead against her temple. He didn't speak for a while, just stood there.

Avery couldn't take the silence any longer. "El?"

His breath fanned across her ear. "I worked hard," he mumbled.

"Worked hard?"

"To get over you," he admitted.

"Oh." *What am I supposed to say to that*? The only thing she could think of was *I'm sorry*. But she didn't say it because it didn't seem like it was enough.

Her stomach clenched in anticipation of his next words. All of a sudden, all of that bravado she'd had a few minutes earlier evaporated into thin air.

"What do you want from me, Avery?" he asked against her ear, before taking her earlobe between his lips.

"Jelly."

"Jelly?" he asked, a chuckle bursting from his lips.

"Oh, goodness," she murmured. "I didn't mean to

say jelly." Jelly was how her legs felt. It wasn't something she'd meant to voice out loud. But the intensity of the moment had apparently fried her brain.
"I mean, you asked me what I wanted from you. My
answer is I don't know. I just…" Avery swallowed
past the hard lump in her throat. "I…"

Somehow, *I'm a chickenshit* didn't sound sexy
or even appealing. But that's exactly what she was.
She was scared out of her mind. But scared of what?
Scared of El? No, she could never be scared of him.
He was everything that was right in her world. He
was beautiful, passionate, intriguing, devoted, sensual…timeless.

Desire pooled in her belly as his lips brushed
down the side of her neck. "If I take you away, will
you let me control where we go and what we do?"

"Yes," she breathed. But what was she agreeing
to, exactly? Avery couldn't think. Hell, she could
barely breathe with him standing so close to her,
being so near her. It was almost like he'd crawled
inside of her, because all she could feel was him, in
every part of her body.

Shaking her head in an effort to clear her mud-
dled brain, she took a step back. "We should probably talk, El."

"I think we've done enough talking, Avery."

"Oh." *Oh? What the*…? She felt his body brush
against hers and braced her hands on his chest. An-
ticipating his touch, his kiss—*what, I don't quite
know*—she clutched the fabric of his shirt in her
hands. "But—" Avery sucked in a sharp breath when
she felt his lips against her mouth.

"You've asked me to take you away. And I have a few conditions."

Swallowing hard, she asked, "What?"

"No work. At any time. I want you with me. All of you. That means, mind clear. No network, no scripts…just me and you."

Avery nodded before she thought better of it. Truth was, it was almost impossible to just be her and him. She'd stalled the network long enough. Jess had just informed her that they'd called ten times that day.

"You don't have to answer me right now," he said, as if he could read her mind. "I know you would have to do a lot to make that happen. So I'm going to leave." Her shoulders sagged in disappointment. "But I'll be back soon."

Then his lips were on her…*forehead*? But damn it, it was the best forehead kiss she'd ever had. Almost as good as if he'd kissed her mouth. Almost.

"I have to get back to the hospital," he said. "We'll talk soon."

She heard the soft click of the door. Avery scooted backward until she felt the edge of the bed against her legs. Then, she sat down.

The quiet he'd left in the room was playing with her. Her mind wouldn't stop spinning, going over every scenario of an extended trip alone with El. Could she really unplug to spend time with him? She didn't know, but she was willing to try.

Chapter 9

El wanted to believe that he was in his right mind when he'd agreed to take Avery away for a few days. But everything pointed to the simple fact that he wasn't.

As a psychiatrist, he was trained to be impassive, to not react. Yet he'd done just the opposite when faced with Avery's plea. *No* would have been the appropriate answer. Instead, he'd agreed with little hesitation.

At this point, he knew they were inevitable. Something was going to happen between them, whether he wanted it to or not. Whether that "something" would make or break them was up in the air.

But Drake had been right when he'd called Avery *his* woman. She'd always been his, from the moment he'd met her all those years ago. Denying that would be denying himself.

When El had been old enough to realize that he had the ultimate control over how he lived his life, it had changed his worldview. It had also changed how he dealt with his brother, his professors, his colleagues. Essentially, he'd vowed to never let anyone take control of his life again.

This realization had happened somewhere around the age of sixteen when he finally accepted the fact that his parents didn't deserve undying love because they'd never given it. And Lawrence would never be the man El had built him up to be in his five-year-old mind. He'd been hurt by the people who were supposed to protect him, but he'd been determined to make the most of his situation.

His parents weren't physically abusive, but it had been hard being the child of two people who wished he wasn't there. If Lawrence hadn't taken him in, who knew where he'd be or what he'd be doing.

Yet, Lawrence was a hard man to live with—even harder to please. He was demanding, manipulative and hypocritical. The expectations Lawrence had set for El and his children had proved to be almost impossible. El had rebelled, and he and Lawrence clashed often. Despite their differences, though, El knew that his brother had saved his life.

Lawrence had given him a chance, the gift of a home. He had nephews and a niece who were more like the siblings he'd dreamed of. They were his bright spot growing up, the reason he was the man he was today. El had managed to make it, to survive. Then he'd met Avery.

El had been somewhat surprised that it had been so easy to fall for her, to open his heart and his soul to her. After everything he'd gone through, he'd fallen hard. He'd let her into a space inside him that, up until then, had been unreachable.

Avery had fed a part of him that was starving and malnourished, filled the void left by his parents and Lawrence.

Those years with her had been the best of his life, and he wanted that back. As wary and hesitant as he was to put himself out there again, he couldn't deny that just being near her again had made him feel more alive than he had in years. And he realized he needed to feel that love.

El was no fool, though. It wouldn't be easy to try with her again, because the trust was damaged, feelings were hurt. But he was willing to try and move forward with her.

His phone's ringtone pierced the quiet of his office and he peered down at his caller ID, smiling when he saw Avery's number.

"Hello," he answered.

"El?"

"Yes, Avie."

"I've thought about what you said."

El sat straight up in his chair. He'd agreed to go with her, but she had to agree to his terms. Would she?

"I'll accept your terms," she continued. "I won't work on the show, but I have some things I'd like to accomplish over the next few days."

El thought about her request for a moment. "This trip is supposed to be about rest, Avie. You can't do that if you're working."

"My foundation," she said. "I'd like to spend an hour each day working on it."

When they were together, Avery had always mentioned starting a nonprofit organization that would help young women of color interested in pursuing science at university. If he remembered correctly, the foundation would not only connect students with mentors already working in math and science fields, but also provide grants or scholarships to students wishing to pursue an education in math and science.

"That's fair," he said. "I think it's great that you want to work on the foundation. I definitely want to support that vision."

"You sound so surprised. I have been talking about doing this for years, El."

"True, but things aren't actually playing out like you'd planned back then."

"Point taken."

There was silence on the other end, so long that El pulled the phone back from his ear to check and see if they were still connected.

Then, finally… "El?"

"Avie," he countered.

In that moment, he felt like she was trying to tell him something important. He couldn't put his finger on it, but he sensed that what she said next would be a game changer.

"I'm sorry."

El closed his eyes, letting her apology wash over him. She wasn't apologizing about anything that had happened since she'd been back in town. This was bigger and rendered him speechless.

"You deserved better than what I gave you, and I'll always regret my choices where our relationship was concerned."

"Why?" he asked before he could stop himself. It was the question that had dogged him for three years.

"I want to have this conversation, El. I do. But not over the phone."

El understood that and wouldn't push. "Okay."

"I wanted to apologize to you because it needed to be said. As cliché and overdramatic as it is, I need you to know that it wasn't you. It was never you."

Avery was right. It was a cliché and the type of thing people said in prime-time dramas or soap operas. It was the kind of explanation that would have sent him into a rage back when the breakup happened. But today it was exactly what he needed to hear.

Avery burrowed back into the passenger seat of El's car as he sped to their destination. Although it had been a few days since he'd last visited, they'd talked daily on the phone. The first call had been from her, when she'd let him know that she agreed to his conditions. The next call had been from him, when he'd told her how to pack and prepare for the trip.

When she'd inquired about where they were going, he'd refused to answer her. That night they'd talked on the phone for over an hour.

It had been years since they'd chatted that way, and it reminded her of when they were first getting to know each other. After they'd met at the Michigan Union Subway, they'd exchanged numbers and had spent hours on the phone chatting about everything from music to science to movies to food.

Avery had only ever been on one date before El. It was her high school prom. Avery had attended

Ann Arbor Huron High School. Huron was one of two public high schools in the area at the time, and one of the best in the state. Shaped like an "H," the school had a wealth of extracurricular activities, clubs, sports and other offerings for their students.

Avery hadn't been a shy teenager, but she wasn't as outgoing as Jess. Jess had been a varsity cheerleader, and ran track. Avery wrote for the school newspaper, *The Emery*. She had also been on the debate team and played flute in the marching and symphonic bands. Some would say she was a nerd, but Avery didn't care. Her activities had kept her busy and her academics were stellar. She'd won several math and science contests that allowed her to meet professors on the University of Michigan staff, which in turn worked in her favor when it came time to apply.

It was one of those teachers, Mrs. Morey, who had convinced her to accept an invitation to prom from a boy in the band. Needless to say, it had been the blind leading the blind. No pun intended. Neither Avery or Matthew had known the first thing about dating and so the prom was a huge dud for her. None of the other boys at school had ever paid her any attention, so she was helplessly inexperienced when she began college.

Sure, she'd met many men on campus, but it was only El who held her attention. They met during her second year, but as far as she was concerned, she didn't need to meet anyone else. He was it for her.

El had been her first kiss, and the first and only man she'd made love to. Feeling a blush creep up her neck, she turned toward the open window. She smelled water outside.

"Are we near Lake Michigan?" she asked.

Avery knew El owned a home near Traverse City. It was one of the things his parents had left him in their will. El had never talked about his parents much. But she did know that he had no relationship with them when they died, many years ago, mere months apart.

"You're so nosy." He laughed softly.

"I'm not telling you where to go. I'm just curious."

"To answer your question, yes."

Smiling to herself, she turned her face toward the window again, imagining the winding roads and the massive lake. Of all five Great Lakes of North America, Lake Michigan was the only one located entirely within the United States and not shared with Canada. The shoreline stretched from Michigan to Indiana to Illinois to Wisconsin. Avery had visited all of the Great Lakes during her lifetime, but Lake Michigan was her favorite. There was something about the shoreline that called to her. She'd often drive there with her parents for day trips. Those were happy times for her, so she always remembered them fondly.

They'd been in the car for a few hours, so she was getting antsy. She wanted to walk, to take in the pure Michigan air. The western side of the state was different than the Detroit metropolitan area, in her opinion. Time seemed to slow when she was away from the city, and she needed that right now. El had always known what she needed.

Avery wondered if they were finally going to have a serious conversation, one about everything that would hurt but would also cleanse. She was finally ready to tell him the truth about why she'd left.

Drawing in a deep breath, she said, "What have you been doing with your life, El? We've seen each other, spent time together. But we haven't really talked about you."

El had never been the type to talk about himself. Avery loved that he was so giving, so willing to shine the spotlight on others, but he'd always been fascinating to her. She wanted to know what he'd been up to.

"It's kind of hard to do that when you're in the middle of a medical crisis," he confessed. "The focus should be on you right now."

"I guess. But why don't we start thinking that I'm on the mend from a medical crisis?"

"I'm glad you said that. I wondered when you would get there."

Avery smiled. "Were you testing me or something?"

"No, but I know you. I knew you wouldn't stay in that depressed state forever. I will admit you had me worried at the hospital."

"Was it the temper tantrums?" Avery wasn't proud of it, but she'd had a meltdown or two in the hospital.

"Not really. It was your look. The despair in your face. Your behavior."

Avery would admit that she was a little hard to deal with. But when faced with the very real possibility of having to learn life again without sight, she'd buckled under the pressure. Now she was ready to pick herself up and do what needed to be done. It helped that she'd been able to do some work, even without her sight.

"I can say that the thought of never seeing my family's faces again still scares me," she admitted softly. "But I'm not dead. I'm still alive, so I still have a chance to get it right, whether I can see or not. I was so distraught, I thought my life was over. The other day, though, I was able to dictate notes on my script and even create a new scene. It wasn't ideal, but it gave me hope that I can do this."

Avery couldn't help but smile at the memory of her and Jess dancing when she'd finished a steamy love scene. She couldn't type it, or even see her words staring back at her on the computer screen. But it was *her* brain that had created it, *her* mind that had dreamed up the scenario.

"I love when you do that."

Surprised that he'd mentioned love when talking about anything she did, Avery asked, "Do what?"

"Be the woman I know you are," he replied. "Now that I'm hearing you say that, I'm not sure you need me anymore."

If Avery could see El, she'd look him in the eye so he could see just how untrue his statement was. She needed him, alright. More than she was ready to tell him at that point. "El, you know I appreciate everything you've done. You didn't have to take time off work and uproot your life to take me away."

El was a busy physician. They'd never talked about what he had to do to get the time off. He'd simply texted to tell her everything was set.

"I didn't uproot my life, Avie. I had time off scheduled in the next few weeks. I just moved it up. A colleague of mine agreed to take over my schedule and my secretary was able to move some things around. We're all good. No work talk, remember?"

Avery did remember. She'd be lying if she said she hadn't thought about work. Jess had sent off the script in her name after they'd worked late getting it done. She'd yet to hear from her boss, but that was okay. She didn't want to hear anything that could possibly ruin this time, this adventure with El.

"Okay, no work talk. Are you dating anyone?" She heard El choke and giggled.

"Seriously, Avie? You just came right out with it, huh?"

"Well, you said no work talk. It's not like we hang in the same circles anymore. I don't know much about your life."

"Do you really think I'd be dating someone and whisking you away for uninterrupted time? Not to mention, I did kiss you."

The kiss. He'd actually mentioned the soul-searing kiss that had left her senses open and her heart beating wildly. "You did do that," she breathed. "But dating someone, or a few someones, does not equate to a committed relationship."

"True," he conceded. "To answer your question, though, I've dated here and there. But no one serious. You?"

"No. I don't have time for dates. I work, sleep, work, eat, work."

"Well, hopefully, you've learned your lesson about that."

"I think so. My main goal right now is the foundation."

"I told you before, I love the idea. Is there a target geographic area?"

"Hell, yeah. Here, my old neighborhood, Ann Arbor, Ypsilanti. Home." For now, she wanted to focus on Southeastern Michigan. The plans weren't mere blueprints any longer. She'd actually made progress on her dream. She wanted to offer the first set of grants by the end of the summer, right before classes started for incoming freshmen. "With the work Jess is doing for the university, she's the perfect person to help me. I've actually considered offering her a permanent job, not that I think she'll take it. She loves her current job."

"Jess is already pretty busy."

Avery thought of her bestie and the devotion Jess had to her career. "I know, but she has that fire I need, El. This project means something to her, too. You should have seen the way her face lit up. I think she'd run with it. Besides, she's the only one I'd trust to run it."

"I will admit she'd be good at it," he said. "Setting up a foundation is a lot of work. You have to be sure you carve out the time to do it."

"I'm not going anywhere for six weeks, at least. That gives us enough time to get some things together."

"Well, let me know if you need help. I'm willing to pitch in."

"I definitely need your assistance as a mentor. While we're away, I want to finalize plans for the fund-raising gala. I'm inviting several people, but I need your help with getting the medical faculty and staff to support."

"Done," he said simply. "What else?"

Frowning, she turned toward him. "What do you mean?"

"Any other changes you plan on making with your life?"

Shrugging, she thought about his question. "I don't know. I guess the proper answer would be to work smarter, not harder. Eat better. Exercise more. Sleep."

He laughed. "What about fun? Don't you want to add that in there somewhere?"

Fun. It had been so long since Avery had fun. The thought made her stomach clench. "I'm not sure I know how to have fun anymore."

"Good thing I'm here to help you."

"What do you do for fun?"

"Nothing."

Avery laughed then. "Straight up? You're lecturing me and you don't bother to have fun?"

"Hey, I'm older."

"By a few years. That doesn't even count. How about I agree to add fun back into my life if you do the same?"

Just then, a flash of light streaked across her eyes, and when she turned toward him she could make out his shadow clearly. Gasping, she brought her hand up to her mouth. And it didn't stop there. She saw him turn to face her. No, she couldn't make out his face, but she definitely made out that movement.

"What's wrong?" he asked.

"I see you," she whispered.

"What do you see?"

She reached out and touched his face, his chin, then brushed her fingers over his cheek. "Not details, but I can see the outline of your silhouette. It's gray. No color, but it's there."

"That's amazing." He held her hand against his cheek and kissed the palm of her hand. "I'm glad."

Avery was afraid to blink, but when she did, he was still there. This time, she could see a fleck of brown in his skin. "Your skin," she breathed. "I can see brown."

After the second blink, though, he was gone. Shoulders slumped, she pulled back. "Gone. You're gone."

He pulled her hand back up to his face. "I'm not gone. I'm still here."

She nodded and wiped a tear from her face with her free hand. "That was amazing."

"That was progress," he said.

El parked the car at the Sleeping Bear Dunes National Lakeshore, close to the Platte River. The park was a tourist spot where people could camp, canoe, kayak, walk along the beach, float on the river, explore the nature trails or climb the steep sand dunes.

"Are we here?" Avery asked.

"We are." He hopped out of the car and jogged over to her door to open it for her. "How does your toe feel?"

Avery hadn't complained much about any pain on their drive. He'd made sure to stop periodically to let her stretch and take a quick walk. The roughly four-hour drive was smooth, since they'd left in the early morning and there wasn't much traffic.

Helping her out of the car, he watched as she tilted her head up to the sun. She wore big designer shades, a pair of khaki shorts and a white tank. Due to her injured toe, she was wearing a pair of sneakers.

"Toe is fine. Where are we?"

El smiled. "We're at the Dunes."

Avery sucked in a deep breath. "Really?"

"Really."

Avery once told him that her family had often visited the park, and she had great memories. When he'd set up the road trip, he'd made it a point to visit places that were dear to her heart. This was the first stop.

He had a picnic basket on dry ice and he'd requested she wear her bathing suit under her clothes so they could go tubing. It was his hope that he could help her hone in on her other senses. After Avery had gotten a glimpse of him in the car, he felt confident that her sight was returning and hoped she'd regain all of it. But even partial blindness was a step forward for her at that moment.

"Can you see me?" he asked.

She lifted her shades to reveal her eyes. "I recognize the sunlight. But it's like everything and everyone is under a gray haze. I see motion, but I can't make out any details."

"That's good." He placed his hand on the small of her back. "There's a spot over there on the beach. I brought us a picnic."

El spread a blanket and steered Avery to the spot once everything was prepared.

Lunch consisted of turkey sandwiches, bottled water and potato chips. They ate in comfortable silence. There were people milling around, kids running along the beach. El enjoyed the serenity and hoped Avery was enjoying it, as well.

"Thank you, El," she said. "You know I love turkey sandwiches."

El laughed. "I almost got ham just to piss you off."

She nudged his shoulder. "You know I hate ham. It would have been World War III here today if you did."

There were two things Avery didn't eat: beans and ham. El could never understand how someone could not like either. He was a fan of both, especially ham. When he was a kid, Lawrence's cook often piled heaping slices of ham on white bread for him for lunch. He could remember gulping the sandwiches down and asking for seconds. The ham was succulent and sweet because the cook made it with a honey-baked crust.

"You know I wouldn't do that to you. I learned my lesson long ago."

"Oh, I remember that day."

El did, too. He'd taken it upon himself to show her the glory of a good ham and brought in lunch from Zingermans, a popular local deli. The sandwiches were the best he'd ever tasted, and he was sure Avery would agree. Except she'd asked for corned beef.

When Avery was studying, she rarely paid attention to anything, even food. He'd set the sandwich in front of her and waited for her to pick it up without even looking at it. One bite and that ham had been plastered to his arm. She'd spit it out immediately, practically choking to get it out of her mouth.

"I still don't know why you have such an aversion to ham. It's so good."

She shrugged. "Hey, I just can't deal with it. I don't even like the smell of it."

She wasn't allergic, she just hated it. After that, El never played with Avery's food again. "Well, I don't want a repeat performance of your food on my arm."

Avery giggled and popped a potato chip into her mouth.

Once they were finished with lunch, El and Avery walked along the beach. Well, he walked and she hobbled.

"Okay?" he asked when he noticed her nose was scrunched up, as if in pain.

"It's kind of hard walking along the beach in shoes," she said. "But I'm a little nervous to take my shoes off. Don't want to step on anything or hurt my toe."

"We can stop here."

There wasn't a lot of traffic on this particular stretch of the beach, which was why he always preferred it. When she sat on the sand, he untied her shoes and pulled them off.

Her low moan of pleasure shot straight to his heart. And his groin. "This is wonderful."

"Lie back," he told her.

"In the sand?"

"Yes."

"My hair?"

El barked out a laugh. "Your hair will be fine.

Here." He took off his baseball cap and placed it on top of her head. "This will help." He slid her sunglasses off.

As Avery slowly lay back on the sand, he thought about how so much time had passed but nothing had really changed as far as his feelings went. He'd meant what he said when he'd told her he'd worked hard to get over her. But he found that he couldn't stop loving her, no matter how hard he'd tried. And he did try. Hard. He'd even employed some of the same tactics he'd taught his patients, to no avail.

"El?"

Lying on his back, he turned his head to view her profile. "Hmm?"

"What are you thinking about?"

"You. Us."

She gasped. "What about us?"

Tracing a finger down her cheek, he said, "About how much I still care."

El had been wanting a reason to not let himself feel what he'd been fighting against since she'd arrived. But he couldn't find one.

"I care, too," she admitted, her voice a whisper. "And the fact that you brought me here, took me away when I needed it, makes me care even more. If that was even possible."

"You should know that there is nothing I wouldn't do for you."

Avery turned to her side and tucked her hand under her face. "El, I'm sorry."

"You already apologized. You don't have to keep doing it."

"I also said there were things we needed to talk about in person. I was wrong. I could've handled things differently. But I thought if I just left, if I hurt you, that was the only way you'd let me go. I was so wrong. And you deserved better from me."

El thought about the months following their breakup with trepidation. Long nights with no sleep, because she wasn't lying next to him. Anxiety had plagued his days for months. He wasn't sure how he'd even lasted a day. Short of begging her to stay, he'd given her every reason to choose him. He'd even hopped on a flight to Atlanta to try and convince her that what they had was worth fighting for. Yet she hadn't fought, and she hadn't chosen him.

A tear streaked down her face and he brushed it away with the pad of his thumb. He didn't want to get into this. He didn't want to relive those moments because he'd worked hard to not let them consume his everyday thoughts. So he told her, "We both made mistakes then. I said some hurtful things, too."

Avery rolled her eyes and muttered a curse, as if frustrated with something. *With me*? "Yeah, I guess."

El knew they were treading on thin ice, so he purposefully steered the conversation back to the present. "What do you hear?"

Avery frowned. "What?"

"I want you to lie still, focus on the feel of the sand in your toes and underneath you. Listen to your surroundings."

Avery closed her eyes.

"What's the first thing you hear?" he asked.

A slow grin spread across her face. "I hear the water, the waves crashing up against the shore."

"Good. What else?"

"The wind. I hear and feel the wind against my face, my legs."

His gaze drifted to her long legs. El was a leg man, and Avery had a pair of legs that had haunted his dreams. Her toes were painted hot pink and she wore a thin silver ankle bracelet. He knew the bracelet had been a gift from Jess when they graduated from high school. Avery rarely took it off. The charm on it said *Sister*. He also noticed a new tattoo on her foot. There were two butterflies.

He sat up and traced the outline of one of them with his forefinger. "When did you get this?"

She shivered under his touch. "About a year ago. Jess and I got them together. The pink one with bursts of blue represents Jess, and the blue with bursts of pink represents me."

That didn't surprise him. Avery's favorite color was cobalt blue. It also didn't shock him that she and Jess had gotten matching tattoos of butterflies, since she loved them. She also had one under her right ear. Avery had told him that she identified with the butterfly because of its metamorphosis. It signified the evolution of the soul and the momentum of life, the fact that everyone grows, evolves and changes. Just like a butterfly.

El took a deep breath, willing his body not to react to her proximity. He wanted nothing more than to kiss her.

"I hear that," she said.

El's eyes snapped to hers. They were still closed. "What do you hear?"

"You're holding back. You want to say something, do something, but you're not for whatever reason."

"What would you say if I told you I wanted to kiss you, but I'm not sure it's a good idea?"

She turned to him then, reached for his face and ran her thumb over his lips. "I'd say do it."

El leaned forward, brushed his nose against hers. "I could never resist you," he murmured against her mouth. Then he captured her lips with his.

Chapter 10

Avery gripped El's shirt in her hands as he kissed her. She felt the steady, firm beat of his heart against her chest as he leaned into her, stealing every bit of breath she had with his mouth.

Once again, he'd rendered her useless for thought. Despite the tranquil surroundings, she was lost in a whirlwind of desire. The serene feeling she'd had only moments earlier had been replaced by a thrill she hadn't realized she'd needed. Yes, she needed the peace he brought, but she also needed this.

A moan escaped from her throat and his hand gripped the back of her head and tilted her so he could gain better access. His mouth was hot, his tongue relentless, his teeth persistent as he nipped at her lips before sucking her lower lip into his mouth.

Passion threatened to overtake her right there on

the public beach, tourists and visitors be damned. Avery didn't care who saw them. She was willing to grant El whatever he wished in whatever way he needed.

Desire pooled low in her belly and she closed her knees to quell the ache between her thighs. His hand pressed low on her stomach, played with the button of her shorts, before sliding down her legs and prying them back open. The feel of his hand brushing over the sensitive skin of her inner thigh had her arching her back up from the sand.

Avery wanted to take his hand, steer it to her slick heat and let him have his way with her. But the faint sound of a child's laughter drifted to her ear and she froze.

El must've heard it, as well, because he pulled back, placing one last kiss at the corner of her lips before retreating. Avery's body was still humming when she felt the soft breeze against her legs.

El tugged her tank down over her belly; Avery hadn't even realized he'd pulled it up. A few more seconds and she would have been shirtless, clad only in her bikini top and shorts.

"Oh, my," she murmured.

From her left, she heard El's deep chuckle. "Tell me about it."

"That was…intense."

El grabbed her hand and placed it over his erection. "Definitely."

Avery smiled, happy that she'd affected him as much as he'd affected her. El was driving her to the brink of crazy. But she hadn't felt so alive in years. They took a few minutes to regain their composure before she turned to him. She could make out his figure.

"El, you are a maniac." She giggled when he barked out a laugh. "I would have let you have your way with me on this beach."

"You wouldn't have."

"Oh, yes, I would have. It's been a long time."

His thumb brushed over her chin. "I find it hard to believe you haven't met anyone you wanted to spend time with."

"Why?"

"You're beautiful, smart...why wouldn't a man try to get with you?"

"I didn't say men haven't tried."

El chuckled. "What about that actor I heard you were linked to?"

Avery grumbled. "Blair and I are not together. We had dinner and the internet blew up. Before I knew it, my face was plastered on the blogs, on Black Twitter. There were memes. Oh, God, it was a nightmare."

"The internet has no chill."

"Blair tried to date me, but I would never date someone like him. He's such an egomaniac. Everything is about him."

"Well, he is an up-and-coming star. I'm sure the decision to cast him is helping your show's popularity. It's like when that medical drama you used to watch cast the young bad boy to play the lead. The show was better for it because he attracted the female audience."

Avery laughed. "No, that show was good because it was well written."

"Yeah, but you can't underestimate the appeal of chemistry between costars, and a good-looking cast."

"How would you know? You wouldn't even watch an episode with me back in the day."

"I've watched a few episodes."

Avery's mouth fell open. "Seriously? After you blazed on me for recording it every week?"

She caught the rise of El's shoulders, before he said, "Netflix."

She relaxed against the cool sand, sucked in a deep breath. "Smell that?"

"What do you smell?"

"Clean. It smells clean here."

El stood up, and she heard the rustle of fabric as he brushed off his clothes. "I rented us several tubes so we could get on the water."

Avery held out her hand and let El pull her to her feet. She couldn't help but be worried about being in the water without really seeing what lay ahead.

El squeezed her shoulder. "Don't worry. You trust me, right?"

Nodding, she said, "Of course."

"Come on."

It took several minutes for them to make it to the river bank. Along the way, El described the sky to her. She couldn't see the blue of it, but according to him, it was clear, with scattered clouds to the west. He then described the water.

His description evoked a childhood memory of her father carrying her to the river bank on his shoulders. Avery had felt invincible because she was taller than everyone.

El tugged at the bottom of her shirt. "You have to take this off."

Avery's face grew warm. "Okay." She pulled her tank off and dropped it on the sand.

Before she could unbutton her shorts, she felt his knuckles graze against her stomach. He unbuttoned them for her and pushed her shorts down. "You can step out of those now."

Avery grinned and did as she was told. Soon they were wading into the water.

El helped her onto the rubber tube. "Don't worry. I've got you," he said when she dug her nails into his arm. "You're not going to float away. I have a tether. You'll be connected to me the entire time."

Avery relaxed a bit. The sound of the current beneath her lulled her mind. She dropped her hand into the water, swirled it around. "This is nice."

"It is."

She felt water hit her face and then heard his laughter. Swooshing water in his direction, she said, "Ha ha. I hope you know you're going to be paying my salon bill."

"Your hair is fine."

Avery wasn't really worried about her hair. Jess had helped her wash and condition it before they'd left. Right now, it was in two double-strand twists.

"How does the water feel?" El asked.

Sighing, she took a minute to breathe in the air on the water and tune out everything else around her. "Warm from the sun. The current is slow, soft, which is surprising because it usually isn't."

"And what do you smell?"

Closing her eyes, she noted the smell of minerals, sand and pine from the nature trails. "Smells like peace."

"Peace?"

"Yes. For the first time in weeks, I feel at peace. And it's because of you."

"I wouldn't say that."

"I would. Really. You took a vacation to bring me here, knowing it would mean the world to me. After everything that's happened between us, it *is* the world to me. It matters."

Avery grinned when El picked up her hand and kissed her palm. "Avie, you don't have to keep thanking me. This is a vacation for me. Time spent with you, away from the hospital is good for me."

Squeezing his hand, she said, "You're good at what you do, you know?"

"Where did that come from?"

"I don't know if it comes natural to you or if you're doing it purposely, but I feel like I can see clear as day here with you. You've described the river, the dunes, exactly the way I remember. You could be a tour guide."

"Yeah, right. Can you imagine me walking around with groups of old women and couples showing them the sights with a smile on my face?"

Avery laughed. No, she couldn't imagine El being so chipper. "Well, now that you put it like that… hell no."

"Maybe when I retire, I'll move up here full-time and spend my days hiking the trails with tour groups."

"Only if you can take your shrink hat off. If not, you'd try to doctor everyone."

"Right. I'd spot all of the sociopaths a mile away. Maybe I'd save the day for some unsuspecting person linked up with a serial killer."

"You're so morbid." Avery giggled. "But you probably would."

El grew quiet, and Avery wondered what he was thinking. "What's next on the agenda?" she asked to break the silence.

"Wouldn't you like to know? It's a surprise."

"I bet I know what it is."

"I'm still not telling you. So just relax."

Avery hoped he was taking her to his house. But she wasn't sure. Either way, she'd roll with it. Every minute with him was a blessing and she'd make the most of it.

El pulled into the long private driveway of his summer home around five o'clock that evening. Avery had once again fallen asleep during the relatively short drive to his house, and he'd been left alone to his thoughts. While on the river, they'd chatted more about her goal for the Avery Montgomery Foundation. He'd offered suggestions on how she could launch it, and given her a few names of faculty who might be willing to help her.

The idea of a foundation to help young women realize their dream of attending college *and* majoring in math, science or pre-medicine was amazing. Avery's parents weren't wealthy. So she knew what it was to work hard and struggle to find funding for college that didn't consist of crushing student loan debt.

Before he'd met Avery, he was admittedly sheltered. He'd rarely been exposed to life outside of the privilege of wealth. El never had to worry about how he would pay his bills. Being with Avery had exposed him to that element. Although her parents were considered middle-class, they couldn't afford her college education. Avery had often struggled to make ends meet, and she wasn't alone in her plight. There were many at the school with similar financial woes.

It made him want to give back to his community. He wanted to make a difference in the lives of those students who weren't as fortunate as he was. So he'd help her in any way he could.

El couldn't believe the way he'd kissed her on the beach that afternoon. One minute he was wanting to kiss her, and the next he was. And now that they were at his house, he wasn't sure what would happen. Being in the car or on a public beach was safer than being alone in the house with a bed, a bathtub and a shower. It wasn't like he could safely pull her onto his lap while he was navigating the streets. And he really wouldn't have taken it too far in broad daylight at the park. Although he'd thought about it several times over the course of the day.

Her smell, like warm shea butter and vanilla, had made him squirm in his seat. And her laughter. He'd missed the sound of her laughter. Avery laughed with her whole body. It started in her throat before it bubbled to the surface. And, like always, everything in him was pulled to her like a magnet to iron. And *damn, my heart…* It beat for her. Only her.

Stopping in front of the house, El leaned his head against the steering wheel. He had a lot of plans for them, for the rest of their short trip. It wasn't going to be easy, being so close to her. But he'd give it a try. Deep down, though, he knew he was a goner.

El froze when he felt the cool tips of her fingers flit over the back of his neck. He turned to her and she was looking right at him. Tilting his head, he gazed into her eyes. "Can you...? Can you see me?"

Avery gave him a slight smile. "I can see your shadow. No color. I'm almost afraid to blink, because I don't want you to go away."

El couldn't help it. He grinned like he'd just won a prize. "If you blink and I'm gone, can you just be okay with that? For now." She drew her fingers back, but he gripped her wrist. "I don't mean be okay with not having your sight. But be patient that this is a sign of good things to come. That you're going to regain your sight. At any minute, it could come back and stay. Focus on your inner healing on this trip. That's what it's for. Okay?"

He could tell she was hesitant, but she nodded. "Okay," she agreed.

El got out of the car and helped her out. He'd called ahead and had his property manager clean and air out the house. The house had been his parents' summer home. It had been left to him after they both died. It was situated on Torch Lake, Michigan's longest inland lake. Located about twenty miles from Traverse City, Torch Lake had become a popular spot for development due to its crystal-clear water. It was an anomaly, in his opinion. There was a Caribbean quality to its water, and because of that, the area was beginning to attract wealthy developers and celebrities looking to purchase the prime real estate on the lake.

Fortunately for him, his parents had bought their

place way before it became the sought-after spot it was now. His father had loved to fish, and the lake was popular for fishing. One of El's first memories was of being on the boat, splashing his feet in the water as his father sat on his big chair with a fishing pole in his hand. It was the only good memory he had of his father, because that trip was the only one he'd been on with his parents before he went to live with Lawrence. So he guessed it was fitting that he remembered it so vividly.

He opened the door and led her in. The housekeeper had left the strong smell of Pine-Sol and bleach in her wake.

"Have a seat," he instructed as he guided Avery over to the sofa. "I want to show you around, but I need to get our things."

Running outside, he made quick work of unloading the car. When he was finished, he locked the door and joined Avery on the couch.

"El?" Her voice was soft, almost unsure. "Is this your home?"

"Yes," he answered.

They'd been here several times, spending many nights sitting quietly on the deck or the small beach or on the boat he owned. He'd brought her there after exam week one year, and it was where they'd made love for the first time.

El knew he was taking a chance immersing them in a place that held so many fond memories, but he knew it was what she needed. She needed to get away—from everything and everyone—for just a little while.

"Do you remember the layout of the house?" he asked.

"Yes. How could I forget? I'm glad you brought me here."

El recalled the way her eyes had lit up when he'd brought her here all those years ago. She'd remarked then that she could see herself living in the house all year round.

Interestingly, El didn't remember how the house had looked when he was younger. But he knew it wasn't as big as it was currently. When the lawyers handed him the deed, he'd traveled up one weekend and found the property in the middle of a massive renovation.

At that time, he'd explained to the contractor who he was and what had happened to his father. Instead of stopping the construction, he'd worked with the builder to finish it, infusing his own personality into the details. The house was beautiful, but his favorite place was the great room they were currently sitting in. The floor-to-ceiling windows, hardwood flooring and warm colors made this a place he could call home.

El stood up, pulling Avery to her feet. As he refreshed her memory of the house, taking her through each of the rooms, he watched her reaction to things. Impressed, he waited as she stepped into each room alone, felt around for the light switch. She'd counted her steps and the doors.

That was the medical student, the doctor, in Avery that he'd loved more than life itself. Once he was done with the tour, she asked him to take her outside to sit on the wraparound porch, which had always been her favorite spot.

Outside, she leaned back in her chair, her face tilted up to the sky and her feet tucked under her bottom.

"I bet the sky is beautiful," she said. "I remember staring at it for what seemed like hours one time we were here."

"Not as beautiful as the person sitting next to me."

El blinked hard. *What the hell*?

"We should probably talk about some things," she said.

"What about?"

"I want to tell you something. It's something I've never told you."

"I have someone bringing dinner in for our first night. Didn't feel like cooking."

She seemed to accept his change in subject when she said, "Okay, that's fine. What time is the food coming?"

El glanced at his watch. "Should be here within half an hour. Do you want to go take a shower or freshen up?"

She straightened in her seat, scooting to the edge and standing slowly. "Sure. Just…follow me. Let me see if I can find my way back."

Once again impressed with her tenacity, he let her walk ahead, followed her to the bedroom he'd designated as hers for their time there.

She stepped inside and turned to the door. "Can you describe the decor?"

El smirked. "I sure can."

The room was painted gray like the rest of the

house, but there was a yellow accent wall. The interior designer had thought the yellow would add a softness to the room for guests, should he decide to rent it out.

El had never really considered renting it out. The place was special to him, to Avery. Aside from letting his nephews come there every so often, he'd kept it for himself.

The queen-sized bed in the center of the room was new. But the interior designer had outfitted it with a gray and yellow comforter set and a mound of matching throw pillows. The wood was a rustic gray color, and a flat-screen television was mounted on the wall.

When they walked into the attached en suite bathroom, he explained that the color scheme of the bedroom flowed into the bathroom, as well. There was also a garden tub and a walk-in shower. "For two," he added.

El smiled at the blush that had begun to work its way up Avery's golden skin.

"For two?" she repeated, with an arch of her brow.

"Shower or bath?" he asked.

"Bath, please."

With his eyes lingering on her small frame, he started the bath, throwing lavender bath salts into the water as it filled the huge tub.

"Did you need help getting your things?"

"I can do it," Avery said, resolve in her voice. "Jess helped me by labeling everything. She used raised stickers on pieces of paper that spell out what it is that I'm touching."

"That's cool," he said. He stopped the water.

"Well, you're all set. I'll leave you alone. But if you need anything, let me know."

"El, actually, I do need something."

"What is it?"

"I need you to answer a question for me."

El hoped it wasn't a deep question. He didn't want to delve into the past. For tonight, he just wanted to be in her company. "Go ahead."

"We've skirted over the issue of us all day. And I just think we should talk about it."

Sighing, El relented. "Okay."

"You mentioned the other day that you didn't hate me. And I just wanted to say I'm glad you don't. I don't think I would be able to make it through this if you did."

"I wanted to hate you," he answered honestly. "Believe me, I tried. I kept telling myself that there had to be more. There had to be a reason why you'd cut us off like you did. I mean, you just walked out on everything we had built together. Yes, your career was taking off when you got the book deal. But I thought you would have at least given me the option to decide for myself what I wanted. The fact that you didn't, that you took my choice away, was especially hard because I've always supported your choices, even when I didn't agree."

Avery bowed her head. "I know," she murmured, her voice shaky. Avery hugged herself, squeezing her eyes shut. "I didn't leave you because I wanted my career over you. I know that's what you think."

"Why would I think anything else? That's what it seemed like. Then again, I don't know. You didn't talk to me. You never said anything. You just ended it."

"This is hard for me. Because telling you the truth would be admitting that I ran scared, that I let someone else dictate my choice."

Confused, El asked, "What does that even mean?"

"I left because of your brother, Dr. Law."

El froze. "What?"

Avery sighed. "Your brother told me that I wasn't good enough for you. He basically harassed me for months, at my job and my house. Eventually, I started believing him. So when the show got picked up, I... ended us."

Chapter 11

Avery stood silent and still after her confession for what seemed like an eternity, unsure of what El was thinking. She knew he hadn't left, because she still felt his presence in the room. She knew he was watching her, trying to figure out if she was telling the truth. But she didn't have it in her to plead her case anymore.

At the end of the day, she was guilty. She'd been the one who broke his heart. And she would be the one who would regret it for the rest of her days.

"Explain," he said, startling her.

Avery went through the story, telling him about the many visits Dr. Law had made to her, the taunts and the offer to pay off her student debt. When she was done, she let out a huge sigh of relief that everything was out in the open.

"Did you take the money?"

It felt like a slap, the accusatory tone in his voice, the question itself. "No," she screeched, grasping at her throat, which had gone dry. "I would never take his money."

"But you did take his advice. You let me go."

"I made a mistake. I let him get in my head." She shook her head. "I should have never let you go."

Yes, Avery had been the one to walk away. But she'd left her heart in the palm of his hand, tucked away and out of her control. There was no one, no other man who could ever hold it. She'd figured out a long time ago that it was just the way it was. Unfortunately, it didn't bode well for her, living hundreds of miles away. But now that she was so close to him that she could smell him, touch him, she felt whole again. Even without her vision, she felt like pieces of her puzzle were falling into place.

"Your bath is getting cold," he said, dousing all of her hopes that this conversation would lead to forgiveness. "I better get ready for dinner."

Then she heard the click of the bathroom door.

Later, Avery and El sat at the dining table eating dinner. The ease they'd had with each other earlier had been replaced with awkwardness. The only sound in the room was the clinking of the silverware on plates, the thud of the glasses on the table. She'd tried to start a conversation several times only to be ignored or answered with one-word responses.

Avery needed to do something fast because the peace she wanted to feel with him was slowly being replaced with dread. It was obvious he was holding back with her, probably because of her blindness. He was angry. He didn't have to say it, she felt it rolling off him in waves. But he'd chosen to hold it in instead of telling her, which infuriated her.

If they stood a chance of getting past the hurt and pain, even if they only ended up friends, they had to start telling the truth. She needed him to treat her like he thought she was the strong woman he fell in love with. Starting now.

"El?"

"What?" he grumbled.

"You want to know how I knew you loved me?"

She heard the rustle of fabric as he shifted in his seat. "How?"

"I knew you loved me because you never sugar-coated things with me. You didn't handle me with kid gloves or treat me like I was some kid who would crumble under the weight of the world. One of the things I noticed early on was that you treated me like an equal."

El had made sure she knew that she could command his attention and hold it. It had made her feel powerful, like a woman. Now he was treating her like everyone else.

"Avery, you—"

"Wait. Let me finish. You're doing it again. You're treating me like everyone else is. I came here with you because I expected you to act normal. Stop making me feel like an invalid. I can't see you, but I can still feel and think and smell. Can you please act like the El I've always known? The man who would tell the truth even if it hurt. *My* El."

"But I'm not *your* El. And you're not *my* Avery.

You haven't been *mine* in years. I don't know what you want me to say."

"I want you to say what you mean and mean what you say."

"Fine. I'm not sure why you want to do this right now, but I'll oblige. When you ended us, it gutted me. Yet I'm here, because maybe I'm a glutton for punishment or something. Because when it's all said and done, when your sight is back and you're healed, you're going to leave. You're going to walk out of here and live your life in your new world with your new people surrounding you and bodyguards everywhere. And I'm going to still be here. Missing you."

"Thank you!" Avery stood, nearly falling back. She didn't dare say that she'd caught a flash of his face during his rant. She didn't want to lose the momentum, didn't want to put a halt to the truth telling that they needed to move forward. "Thank you! That's what I need. Tell me how much I hurt you because I know that I did. I hurt myself when I left you. There isn't a day that goes by that I don't think of you and wonder what you're doing."

"I still don't know how this will help the situation," he hissed. "Telling you how I feel is counterproductive."

"I need the truth. You need to tell me so that it's out in the open and not bottled up. But you won't do that because you're treating me like I'm sick, like I'm near death. You're holding back and you never have before. You didn't at the graduation. Treat me like I just walked back into your life and can see you."

Because she could. She could see him. Not every part of him, only one eye and one ear. Avery could see his brown skin and fought the urge to run to him and smooth her hands over the defined muscles she knew lay underneath his shirt. He was the most beautiful thing she'd ever seen.

"Avery, stop."

"No, I won't stop. I'm not just anybody. I'm not one of your patients. I'm Avery freakin' Montgomery. Act like it. Act like I'm strong and can handle your truth, act like I'm capable of taking it, like I can walk over to you and smack you in the face and not even bat an eye." She walked toward him and stopped in front of him. "Then…" She let out a shaky breath. "I need you to make love to me."

Up close, she could see the lines of his face, the wide set of his eyes. "What?"

"I don't care what happened. I don't even care what's going to happen. But I almost died. I haven't felt like myself in years. Not until I saw you in the back of that auditorium. Not until I talked to you. Not until you kissed me at the park and on the beach. You've brought feeling back into my body, heat back into my heart. I need you to do it again. And not in a sad, pitiful, feel-sorry-for-me kind of way. I need you to do it the way you've always done it. I need you to be *my* El."

"You just walked over here," he whispered, a soft smile on his lips. A smile that she knew was there because she could see it. "You're looking at me like you can see me."

"That's beside the point."

Avery didn't want to jinx it. She didn't know how long it would last. As it was, her vision was like streaming a movie when the connection was slow. One minute he was there, the next he wasn't.

"Actually, it's not," he countered. "You can see me."

She blinked and he disappeared, just as fast as he'd appeared. This time, though, she could still make out his lean frame, his stance. "I *could* see you." She felt tears welling up in her eyes. "For a minute, I could see your eye, your skin."

"And now?"

She shook her head. "You're just a shadow again."

He ran his hand down her cheek and gripped her chin in his hand. Pulling her to him, he met her lips with his in a searing kiss. Avery fell into him, wrapping her arms around his body as he devoured her like she was his last meal. His tongue slipped past her lips and she opened willingly, offering him every bit of herself with that kiss.

When El pulled back, Avery was still wrapped in a haze with her eyes closed and her mouth open. She wanted more, needed more.

El stepped away from her and she immediately missed his warmth. "El," she murmured. "Please, don't stop."

"Take that dress off."

El stared at Avery, standing before him. Her skin was flushed and her breathing was erratic. She was glorious, as beautiful and captivating as she'd been when he first met her. He'd been immediately drawn to her then, as he was now.

"Take it off. The dress."

Avery blinked and her mouth fell open. "What?"

"You heard me. Take it off," he repeated. "Now."

"Don't."

"Don't what?" He circled her like she was his prey, taking in the way she looked in the midnight-blue halter dress. It was low-cut in the back, showing him all the skin he needed to let his imagination run wild. He couldn't wait to see it lying in a puddle under her feet.

Despite his good intentions, he wanted her. And since she'd asked, he'd give it to her.

"El, wait. I—"

"Oh, no, Avie. You were all big and bad a few minutes ago. You want me to give it to you straight? How about I just give it you. All night."

Avery swallowed visibly, her hand flying to her throat.

"What's the matter? Scared?"

Her confession that his brother had something to do with their breakup had pissed him off to the point where he'd briefly considered driving back to Ann Arbor and kicking Lawrence's ass. But El knew that wouldn't help the situation. This would, though. It would help both of them.

And despite his arguments to the contrary, he'd always known how he felt. Whether she was near or far, he always wanted to be wherever she was. He doubted it would ever change.

Moving closer to her, he looked into her eyes, saw the fresh sheen of tears in them. There would be no one else for him. Tomorrow might be different, but today—tonight—was theirs.

When she still didn't move, he walked behind her and untied the halter behind her neck. Leaning down, he placed a soft kiss on her nape.

El dropped the straps, exposing her breasts to his hungry eyes. "You're so beautiful." He hooked an arm around her waist, pulled her against him and whispered, "You told me that you wanted me to treat you like you're *my* Avery, correct?"

Avery nodded.

Taking her earlobe in his mouth, he bit down on it until she cried out his name. El pushed her dress down, and turned her to face him. "I don't hear you, Avie. Use your words."

"Yes."

Fueled by her soft admission, he lifted her up and carried her through the house to his room, enjoying her surprised yelp and delighted laughter.

Avery had told him that she hadn't dated anyone, but his goal tonight was simple. He wanted to brand her, sear her with his love so that she knew he was the only man that would ever make her feel the way he did.

Inside his bedroom, he set her on her feet. "Avie?" He pinched her chin and smiled when her lips parted for him. "Show me what you need from me."

Lifting up on the tips of her toes, she met his mouth in the lightest of kisses. "El, I just need you."

The tiny contact coupled with the desire shining back at him through her eyes did him in. It was over for him, and he wanted more. Framing her face with his hands, he kissed her long and hard. El had never wanted to possess any woman before Avery. He wanted to take care of her, give her what she needed.

El couldn't stop touching her. His fingers moved over her earlobes, skimmed her bared shoulders then down her sides. "Beautiful," he murmured against her mouth before capturing her bottom lip in his.

Avery whimpered when he broke the kiss, blazing a trail of open-mouthed kisses down her neck and between her breasts before taking one of her pebbled nipples into his mouth. She dug her nails into his shoulders as he sucked and nipped at her skin.

El resisted the urge to mark her, to leave evidence that he'd been there. Not that it mattered, because he'd already decided that no one else would ever experience her that way.

He gripped her hips in his hands and placed more kisses over her collarbone and across her stomach. On his knees, he dipped his tongue into her navel. Hooking his thumbs in the waistband of her lacy panties, he slid them off.

He ran his hands over her ankles and up her legs before urging her legs apart. Continuing his mission, he kissed her pelvis, down the front of her thighs and knees. Placing kisses over her inner thigh, he inhaled her sweet scent before he touched his tongue to her womanly core.

His name on her lips propelled him further, and he continued, rubbing his thumb over her clit before taking it into his mouth and sucking until her knees buckled and she cried out her release. Oh, but he wasn't done. Not yet, not when she tasted so good, so sweet.

Avery was leaning against him, her hands planted on his shoulders as the remnants of her orgasm shot through her. Unable to resist, he slid a finger through her slick folds before he took her in his mouth again. This time, he pushed a finger inside her, then two.

"Please," Avery begged. "I'm going to fall."

"I'll never let you fall," he murmured against her skin before curving his fingers inside her and hitting the spot that sent her careening over the edge of bliss again.

Her sharp intake of breath had him looking up at her. She was looking down at him, her eyes on his.

"El," she breathed, brushing her fingers over his forehead, over his eyelids, down his nose, across his lips. "I can see you."

Chapter 12

Avery was so overcome with emotion, a tear fell. The sight of El, clear as day, on his knees worshipping her body, nearly took the wind out of her. Dropping to her knees, she let him pull her into a hug.

He rubbed her back, whispered words of comfort to her. "You're okay, baby," he said. "I've got you."

"El," she cried. "I saw your face."

Pulling back, he held her face in his hands. "And now?"

"You're blurry, but still there."

Still awed by his appearance, by his presence, she traced the line of his nose with her finger, then his lips, gasping when he took her finger into his mouth, flicking the tip with his tongue.

Avery leaned into him. "Thank you," she said, hugging him tightly.

To be treated to a delicious, consuming orgasm and open her eyes to the vision of him in front of her was one of the best moments of her life. It made her want to write, to capture the moment on paper. But she'd keep her promise to him about not working.

"El?" she called softly, suddenly concerned that the return of her vision and her subsequent emotions had changed the tone of the evening. She still wanted him; she wanted to continue their lovemaking.

"Hmm?" he murmured.

"Make love to me?" she asked.

Taking her hand in his, he kissed her fingertips. She was naked, and he was fully clothed. Time to remedy that. Before he could answer, she lifted his shirt off. Allowing herself a moment to feel him beneath her hands, she sighed as a wave of pleasure washed over her. He was real, he was warm and for tonight he'd be hers again.

Avery didn't fool herself into thinking that one night would magically solve their problems, but she hoped it would be a start. She had every intention of seeing it through, making the effort to salvage what they had.

El was like her personal angel, sent from heaven just for her. From the moment their eyes met all those years ago, she'd felt the connection. She'd likened it to an internal explosion because of its intensity. Distance and time, hurt feelings and misunderstandings, had done nothing to temper the overwhelming feelings of need, desire, lust…love she felt when she was near him. She wanted to revel in that feeling.

She ran her fingers through his hair. El leaned his forehead against hers before kissing her gently. Soon the kiss turned frantic. She unbuckled his belt and pulled it off, tossing it behind her head. Unable to break the kiss, she unbuttoned his pants and pushed them over his hips.

His fingers slid over her, drawing a low moan from her. She was on fire, burning for his touch, craving him inside her.

He stood, pulled her up to her feet. Laying her back on the bed, he kissed his way up her body until he'd nestled himself between her legs.

Kissing her chin before nipping it lightly, he said, "Are you sure, Avie?"

Avery wanted to see him more clearly, but she was just happy she could see at all. The dim lighting in the room cast a warm glow over his skin that almost made him seem luminous, golden. If she were an artist, she'd put him on canvas, he was so beautiful. She felt him, hard against her opening.

"I'm very sure," she said.

El slid inside her, filling her up so completely Avery closed her eyes against the gamut of emotions that coursed through her. He held still, his head dropping to her neck.

"Damn," he muttered, before biting down gently on her shoulder. "You feel so good."

Cradling him with her legs, she hugged him close to her. "So do you."

They stayed like that for a while, just enjoying the connection, the feel of each other. Soon, he pulled out and then slowly pushed himself back in. She felt his lips on her neck, his tongue sliding across her skin.

"You taste good," he murmured against her skin. "I can't get enough of you."

Avery's eyes fluttered closed. She knew the feeling, because she felt it, too. It had always been like this between them. They'd been compatible on every level, which was why she hadn't hesitated to give her virginity to him. He knew her body better than she did, could bring her to completion with well-placed kisses and hot words. El was a generous lover, never failing to give her what she needed.

He'd taught her everything she knew about the art of lovemaking, had inspired many love scenes in her writing. She'd been a willing pupil, too. Running a finger over his spine, she wondered what he was going to teach her tonight.

"Baby," he said, looking at her.

Smiling up at him, she tried to focus on the outline of his face. "Yes?"

"Tell me we'll be okay."

Avery blinked. There was something so sweet, so vulnerable about El's statement. He wanted her to reassure him. It was a switch for them, because he'd often been the one who was in control of his emotions throughout their relationship. To hear him ask her to tell him that they would be okay made her want to promise him the world in that moment. Logically, she knew there were no guarantees, but that didn't stop her from wanting to make everything good for him.

Cupping the back of his head, she pulled him to her, placing a lingering kiss on his lips. "We're going to be okay. No matter what."

El buried his face in her neck as he moved inside her, picking up the pace. Avery met his powerful thrusts with a fire of her own. The only sounds in the room were those of skin against skin. There were no groans, no moans, just them, communicating with their minds.

A frenzy took over, and she clung to him, wrapping her legs around his waist in an effort to bring him closer still. He pushed himself up on his knees, picking her up in his arms. She rode him, undulating against him until she felt herself unravel.

"Close," she said, struggling to catch her breath.

"Let go," he commanded. "I'm right with you."

He sucked her bottom lip into his mouth and the thin band of control she had left snapped. They climaxed together, each groaning the other's name.

Avery fell back against the mattress, smiling when El pulled her against his side. It was something he'd always done after they made love. He'd once told her that it was because he needed to feel close to her, needed to still feel the connection.

Her life hadn't been perfect by a long shot, even before her stroke. But being there with El, feeling his presence was as close to perfection as she could ever hope for. Fame and notoriety hadn't been enough. Her life was incomplete without him. Even if this lasted for only a little while, her feelings for him would last an eternity.

Avery wanted to say something, but she didn't want to break the spell. She didn't want to do anything that would jeopardize the harmony they'd created. Closing her eyes, she relaxed into him.

Avery traced the lines of his muscles in his thighs and his abdomen, naming them in her head. *I'm such a nerd.*

"Which muscle is that?" he quizzed her, picking up on her thoughts.

When Avery was taking anatomy during her undergraduate third year, El would test her knowledge on his body. Swiping her finger over his upper thigh, she said, "Sartorius muscle." She smoothed her hand upward, settling it on his stomach. "And this is the rectus abdominis, better known as the six-pack."

He chuckled, and it was music to her ears.

"El—"

"Avie—"

She giggled. "You go ahead."

"No, you go."

"I don't regret tonight," she blurted out. "I hope you don't."

He hugged her tighter. "I don't, Avie. I am concerned that we kind of skipped over a lot of things to get to this point. We haven't really solved anything. But regret? Nah. I think we both needed this."

She laughed. "Understatement of the year?"

El pulled her on top of him, and she straddled his hips before sitting upright. He sat up, as well, running his thumb along her spine. "Is that your way of telling me you were burning with need for me?"

Tracing his upper abdomen and his shoulders, she once again ticked off the muscle names in her head.

"Name it," he ordered as her hand slid over his shoulder.

"Trapezius," she answered. "And 'burn for you' is romance talk. I write drama and scandal with a dose of humor." When he barked out a laugh, she joined him. "But to answer your question..." She kissed his shoulder blade. "I want seconds."

Avery awoke the next morning and said a prayer before she opened her eyes. Unfortunately, her vision hadn't gotten any better. But it wasn't worse. She could still see, albeit partially.

She didn't need to see to know that El wasn't in the bed next to her. His side of the bed was cold, as though he'd been gone for a while. Sighing, she sat up and leaned her back against the headboard. She couldn't hear anything. The house was quiet. No television, no running water…nothing.

It wasn't like El to leave her during the night, but she also hadn't been with El in a long time. Change wasn't out of the realm of possibility. He'd told her he wasn't dating anyone but she'd be naïve to think he'd stayed celibate just because she wasn't around.

El was a sexy man, and she was sure women had offered him their company with little effort from him. Avery rubbed her face, unwilling to bring the thought of other women into the moment they'd shared.

A headache settled right between her eyes, and she couldn't help the concern that plagued her thoughts. All of this had started with a headache. The worst headache she'd ever had. Even now, she could remember the debilitating pain. Her attempts to work right through it had only made it worse.

A chill racked her body, and she pulled the cover over her. *Where is he?*

"You're up," El said from the doorway.

Avery's gaze flashed over to him. He was a sight for worried eyes. "You're here?"

"Where else would I be?" He walked over to the bed, ran a finger over her creased forehead. "How are you this morning? Any improvement in your vision?"

"Same, but it's a good sign."

El smoothed a hand over her hand, leaned down

and placed a sweet kiss on her mouth. "It's more than good. It's amazing."

Swallowing, Avery scooted over when he sat on the edge of the bed. "You weren't here when I woke up, so I didn't know what to think."

"I couldn't sleep," he confessed. "So I decided to read."

"What are you reading?"

"A psychological thriller about two brothers who go back to their childhood home and discover hidden secrets."

"Ah," Avery said. "Will you read to me? I haven't read a book in a while."

El caressed her face and pulled her into an intense kiss. "I will tonight. But you need to get dressed. I have plans for us."

Avery pouted. "What if I want to stay here and rest? Isn't that what this trip is about?"

"That and so much more. Trust me, you'll love where I'm taking you today."

Around noon, Avery and El pulled up at a local Italian eatery. When the host showed them back to a private dining space, she gasped at the smell of flowers that filled the room and the scented candles. "Oh, my God, this is heaven. Where did you find this place?"

"I have connections. Have a seat."

Avery sat at a small table in the center of the room. Slowly, she'd been able to make out more of her surroundings, but she still struggled with details going in and out. She did realize fairly quickly that there was no one else in the restaurant. They were alone.

"I know this is a private dining room, but where are all the people?"

"The restaurant is closed. It's just me and you."

Avery's mouth fell open. "Really? In the middle of the week? Do you know the owners?"

"I do. They are old friends of my family. Now be quiet." He sat next to her. "I know you love flowers so I had them bring them in just for you. I also took the liberty of ordering our lunch and dessert."

Avery moaned when she caught a whiff of lilacs. The flickering light of candles basked the room in a warm glow. The host entered with a bottle of chardonnay and poured a full serving in each wine glass before excusing himself.

Inhaling the scent of the wine, she caught notes of vanilla, butter and coconut. "Yum," she murmured before taking a sip. Avery loved the citrus flavor paired with the butter and vanilla. It was simply delicious. "It's lovely."

"I figured you'd enjoy it," El said.

The server arrived a short time later with lunch—chicken marsala, garlic mashed potatoes and sautéed spinach. As the smell of mushrooms and sauce filled the room, Avery glanced up at El. "This is heavy for lunch."

"Dinner is light, so I figured it would be best to eat a hearty meal now."

Shrugging, Avery sliced the chicken breast with her knife and slid a piece into her mouth, groaning at the succulent taste. "This is amazing, El."

As they ate lunch, they chatted about the restaurant's origins. Avery was surprised that the owner was an African American man. El explained that he was a long-time friend of his brother, a doctor who had retired to the area to open up the restaurant. It had been a personal goal of the older gentlemen to use his late Italian grandmother's recipes for good. And after years putting in hard work as a physician, he'd made the move with his family.

"He has four daughters," El said. "One of them is good friends with Ian."

Avery nodded. "How is Ian?" she asked.

She'd grown quite close to El's nephews and niece over the years. She missed them, and had often wondered how they were doing.

"Ian is Ian. He's planning to volunteer with the American Red Cross during the summer, down in New Orleans. I'm proud of him for stepping away from Lawrence's sphere of influence."

El's brother's name sent a chill down her spine and she wondered how the man would react to her being back in town. Did he even know? "That's amazing. I always knew he'd do something totally surprising."

"It's so odd how different he and Myles are."

"And Myles? What is he up to?"

"Myles is planning to secure a fellowship at UCLA. I think he has a good shot, too."

Avery always knew Myles had been the serious twin. He was dedicated to his career goals and rarely strayed from the path dictated by Dr. Law.

"When does Mel graduate?"

El smiled at the mention of Mel. Avery recalled how he doted on her when they were together. She was much younger than her brothers and the product of Dr. Law's third wife. Needless to say, the older man got around. It still burned her up that he'd had the nerve to judge her.

"Mel graduates next spring."

"Medical school?"

El shrugged. "I don't think so, although Lawrence is pushing for it. Last we spoke, she mentioned she was interested in Higher Education. She spent the last semester as a teaching assistant for one of her chemistry professors, and she enjoyed it."

"I still can't believe Drake married Love," Avery said, changing the subject. "When he told me that, I was floored. How in the world did that happen?"

Love and Drake had been best friends since they were toddlers. They'd always firmly eschewed any mention of romance between them, so it was a shock to hear that they were married and happy.

"Trust me, it was a surprise for us, too. You should have seen him running around the hospital all crazed."

El then told her the story of Love and Drake waking up in a hotel room, naked and married. When he was done, Avery gaped at him. "That's crazy."

"But they're good together. You know, Love is the only woman who can handle Drake. They get along well, and they love each other fiercely. To think they almost let it go, like…"

"Like we did?" Avery said softly.

"Avery, you have to know I've never stopped loving you."

Nodding, Avery considered his admission for a moment. "I know you love me, El, but does it matter to you anymore? Sometimes people and things get in the way, and those things take the feeling out of love. The shell is still there, but the feeling is gone. Get what I mean?"

"I do."

"I don't think you've magically gotten over my leaving. I know you want to. I can feel it when you're with me. It's like you're conflicted." Avery knew there was no time jump to the past or the future to fix their problems. But she hoped he was willing to truly try. She placed her hand on his and squeezed. "I want you to forgive me, to trust me again. With your heart. I want you to feel safe with me, the same way I've always felt with you."

"Avery, I—"

Avery placed a finger over his mouth. "Don't say you trust me, because I know that you don't. And that's fine. I understand. And I'm willing to wait because I've realized something over the past few weeks."

El raised a brow. "And that is?"

"You said you tried hard to get over me, but I know for certain I can never get past loving you. It's just a fact of my life, and there's no sense in denying it anymore. I want you, El. I want us back, and I'm going to work for it, for you. I love you."

Chapter 13

El let out a slow breath he didn't know he'd been holding. It was one thing to know Avery loved him, but quite another to hear her tell him she was willing to fight for his love.

"Maybe it's hard for you to believe," Avery continued. "Especially considering our past. But it's the truth. I will go to my grave with this love for you. I love you more today than I did yesterday. I'll love you more tomorrow than I did today."

Avery had laid her feelings out on the table for him to dissect or even throw back in her face. The fact that she'd done so without even batting an eyelash made his heart hammer in his chest.

Yet, he wasn't sure what to say. Those three words would have brought him to his knees had he been standing. Hell, yes, he was being dramatic. But he didn't care. He wanted her, open for him on that table right now.

"Let's go," he said.

Avery's eyes widened. "What? I'm not done."

"We'll have it boxed up."

"El?"

"Avery, if we don't leave right now, I'm going to have you on this table, in this restaurant right now."

She reared back in her seat before she jumped up, nearly knocking her glass to the floor. El watched her finish her wine and quickly led her out of the restaurant, food and dessert be damned.

The car ride home was hard. He was hard. And Avery wasn't playing fair. She'd scooted closer to him and was currently kissing, biting and sucking every piece of exposed skin he had.

Groaning, he shook his mind clear so he could concentrate on the road ahead. But when her hand brushed over his strained erection, he nearly lost control of the car, jerking the steering wheel to the right to keep from running the car off the road.

Still, Avery didn't stop there. She unzipped his jeans and pulled his hard length out. *Shit.* Before he could stop her, her warm mouth was on him.

When he spotted the driveway, he whipped the car into the driveway and immediately put it in Park. She was persistent, the little minx. She didn't seem to care they were in the car or that he could have very well crashed into a pole or something. She barely missed a beat as she pleasured him, bringing him to the brink of orgasm with her hot mouth.

Unable to take it any longer, he pulled her off him

and over the console to his lap. Straddling him, she lifted her dress up. He rubbed her sex through her thin panties before ripping them off. Then she lowered herself onto him and El gave in to the urge to close his eyes. She felt good, and he felt dizzy with a frenzied need for completion.

He heard the buzz of the seat lowering before he felt the descent. She'd thought of everything. Gripping her hips, he arched below her, pushing himself into her hard. Her cry was music to his ears, and he wanted to hear it again. Lifting her up, he slammed her down on him again.

"Oh," she gasped before she started moving against him, grinding into him as if her life depended on it.

They moved in sync, each of them racing toward the orgasms they both needed. There was no sound, not even a groan. Her eyes…her open and *seeing* eyes were on his. Framing his face in her hands, she brought his mouth to hers in a bruising kiss. Their lips were firm, their tongues searching.

When she pulled back, her eyes rolled into the back of her head and she rode him. Tugging the top of her dress down, he took one of her nipples in his mouth, sucking hard until she finally let out a whimper. Avery's head fell back as her eyes fluttered closed. He was having none of that, though. He wanted to watch her; he wanted her to see him when she climaxed.

Wrapping a gentle hand around the back of her neck, he pulled her back to him, kissing her before he said, "Keep your eyes open, Avie. On me."

Avery's eyes popped open, dark with desire. Then she climaxed, his name tumbling from her mouth over and over. One more thrust and he was done, coming so long and hard he briefly wondered if he would lose his mind. The intensity of it stole his breath, and the only word he managed to get out was her name, "Avie."

Avery slumped against him, and El wrapped his arms around her. They stayed like that for a few minutes, him struggling to catch his breath and her breathing heavily.

When she sat up, looking down at him with hooded eyes, he couldn't help the smile that spread across his face. He moved a strand of hair from her face. She'd worn it curly and wild when they left the house. Now it was limp and sticking to her face. But she was still the most beautiful woman he'd ever laid eyes on.

He placed kisses on her cheeks, her nose, her brow, then her lips. He swatted her behind, laughing at her surprised yelp. "We have to get out of the car."

Avery covered her face and dropped her head onto his shoulder. "I can't believe we just did that."

"We've done worse."

There had been a time when they couldn't keep their hands off each other. They'd christened every room in his house and her apartment, his car, her car and even the hospital.

"You're right." She scraped his scalp with her fingernails before she sat up. "You're beautiful," she whispered, rubbing her thumb over his bottom lip before she placed a sweet kiss there.

"I think you're the only person that has ever called me beautiful."

She frowned. "Well, you are."

"I'm not sure how I should feel about that."

El had been told he was handsome, cute, mysterious, good-looking, but never beautiful. And it had never bothered him before because he'd been taught that "beautiful" was something you called a woman or a work of art. The fact that Avery thought he was beautiful intrigued him.

"Why beautiful?" he asked.

Avery graced him with one of her gorgeous smiles. "Because. You're like a timeless piece of art. Your face, your body, your mind. Everything about you is beautiful."

"I feel the same way about you."

Ducking her head, she pushed at his shoulder. "Stop."

Avery had never felt comfortable with compliments. It was for that reason that he liked to shower her with them. She never expected it, which made it fun for him.

El squeezed her thighs, "Come on. Let's get cleaned up."

"I quit, El. You're cheating."

Avery pinned El with a heated gaze. Her vision was holding steady. As each hour passed, she could make out more details.

"How can I cheat?" he asked, a smirk on his lips. "I'm rolling the dice just like you are."

"But you have all the good properties."

"It's not my fault you keep going to jail. Maybe you're just not that lucky."

"I don't have any more money. All I have left are stupid ones and fives."

El laughed. "Don't blame me because you can't manage your money. You shouldn't have gone berserk buying up all those properties. This is supposed to be a game of strategy."

Avery rolled the dice, groaning when she landed on Boardwalk. Throwing her money down, she stood. "I'm done."

"Still a sore loser, huh?"

"I don't recall you liking to lose either, El."

El stood and approached her, wrapped his arm around her waist and pulled her flush against him. "Since you're obviously giving up, I win. Remember the deal."

Avery rolled her eyes. "I remember the deal, damn."

El held out his hand, a wide grin on his face. "Pay up."

Crossing her arms across her chest, Avery frowned. "You bought them for me. Why should I give it to you?"

"Because that was the deal."

Avery muttered a curse and handed El the last cookie. "No fair."

"We can share," he said with a wink. "I'll break it in half."

Avery grabbed the cookie and turned around, limping away as fast as she could, knowing he'd catch up to her because her toe still hurt a little. It took him two-point-two seconds to snatch her off her feet and sling her over his shoulder.

"El," she laughed. "Put me down."

"Give me that cookie."

They'd spent the rest of the afternoon in bed, enjoying each other. El had arranged for a dinner of desserts. A caterer had delivered a bunch of different choices—tiramisu, chocolate cake, apple pie and peanut butter cookies.

They'd saved the cookies for last, because they were her favorite. Avery swore the caterer was a magician because the cookies were almost better than her aunt Nora's peanut butter cookies—soft, gooey and full of flavor.

Avery laughed as El tickled her sides, then...*tragedy*. The cookie fell. "No!" she shouted.

The last perfect cookie hit the floor with a soft thud. El looked back and muttered a curse. "Aw, man. That sucks." He set her to her feet. "I'm sorry."

She pushed him playfully and bent down to pick up the cookie. "Now what are we going to eat?" Avery tossed the cookie into the trashcan. "You were so hell bent on getting out of the restaurant, we didn't bring back my leftovers."

"There's food here. I'll make you something to eat."

"So I can die?"

El laughed. "Ha-ha. I hope you know I've learned a thing or two about cooking. I fed Drake for days while Love was out of town."

Avery wrapped her arm around his neck and kissed him. "You're so cute when you're defensive."

Their gazes locked. El leaned down, resting his forehead against hers. "This is perfect."

With El's hands splayed low on her back, he slowly started swaying them back and forth. Avery couldn't help the tears that welled up as they danced to a music all their own, a rhythm only they could hear. *Perfect* was the right word. He was *her* perfect El.

His voice was soft at first, and Avery hummed when it registered that he was singing their song. The very first time they'd slow danced it was to Luther Vandross's *Because It's Really Love* at the Black Student Union's annual eighties party. He'd sung to her then, too. It was also the first time she realized she'd fallen in love with him.

El's baritone voice was soft in her ear as he sang. The words took her breath away then because she knew they'd rung true for him then, and they did now. That song had been one of her favorites because it reminded her of her father and long car rides to exciting destinations. Vandross was one of her father's favorites so she grew up on his music. But after that dance, every time she heard the song it brought back the memory of that party, that dance, *her* El.

Avery raked her nails over his scalp and lifted herself up on her good toes. "I can't thank you enough." She brushed her lips over his before deepening the kiss.

With his hand braced against the back of her head, holding her to him, Avery couldn't have moved if she tried. Which she didn't. She savored the feel of his mouth on hers, the thrill of his tongue stroking hers. It wouldn't take much for them to be in the throes of passion again, especially since she was wearing one of his oversized T-shirts and nothing else.

Breaking the kiss, El embraced her. "Perfect," he murmured before placing a gentle kiss on her brow.

Even though they still had a lot to work through, Avery knew that they'd just turned a corner and prayed that when they left their little haven they'd be able to face whatever came their way together.

Chapter 14

Back in Ann Arbor a few days later, Avery and El walked hand in hand into the hospital for her follow-up appointment. Their little vacation had been pure bliss for her.

The rest of the trip had been spent exploring the area during the day and each other at night. And even though her sight had consistently improved, he still helped her hone in on her other senses. He'd planned a boat ride on Torch Lake, a visit to a vineyard for a private wine tasting, complete with a decadent raspberry torte that made her toes curl it was so good.

For the first time in years, they were in sync, totally enveloped in each other. She wouldn't trade the time they'd spent together for anything.

Realistically, she knew they still had an uphill battle before them, but she'd meant what she told him. She was willing to fight for them.

When they arrived at the clinic, she checked in and took a seat next to El. He was scrolling through his phone. "Everything okay?"

"Yeah," he murmured, tapping at his screen.

El had contacted neurology on their way back and asked that she be seen that day. While most of her sight had returned, she was still experiencing some depth-perception problems. One evening, she'd almost broken her neck when she underestimated the number of stairs and took a tumble down a short flight.

He'd wondered if there might be some residual damage that would benefit from therapy. Initially she'd resisted the thought, arguing that she was too busy to have to go to the hospital every day to do things she could do at home.

They'd compromised on the visit today, but she was sure they'd argue about it more later when she told him she was done with appointments after this one. It wasn't that Avery was being ornery, but she'd had enough of doctors, nurses, MRIs, CT scans and lights in her eyes. The miracle that her sight was back at the point where she could read and write again made her want to seize the day—not spend it at Michigan Medicine. She'd rather be back in his house, lazing on the beach with him.

"You think you'll be okay here by yourself for about twenty minutes?" he asked.

"Sure," she replied. "You're sure you're okay, right?"

"I'm fine, Avie. Just checked my emails and saw something that concerned me about one of my patients. I just want to check in with my colleague about the case."

Avery nodded, leaning forward and letting him place a kiss on her brow.

"I'll be back shortly."

After he left, Avery tapped her hands against her legs. Nervous energy filled her, and she wanted to call Jess. But she'd left her cell phone at home.

She considered asking a nurse if she could use the clinic phone but decided to wait. When the medical assistant called her name, Avery stood up and hurried to the back when a few of the people in the lobby started staring at her. Back to reality, back to the possibility of someone recognizing her face or her name.

As she followed the nurse to the exam room, she noticed a group of doctors conversing. After checking her vitals, the nurse asked for an autograph. Avery obliged and relaxed into her chair once she was alone.

Outside the room, she could hear two women talking. Nothing abnormal, mostly gossip about doctors and nurses. When she heard El's name, though, she perked up.

"Have you talked to him lately?" she heard a woman ask. "I just saw him a few minutes ago looking fine as ever."

A tinge of jealousy flared in Avery at the woman's description of El. *Her* El.

"No, he hasn't reached out," another woman answered.

Curious, Avery leaned forward.

"You should call him, Lana."

Lana. Who the hell was she?

"No, Hailey. El just isn't ready. We went out a few times, double dates with Love and Drake, but he...he was pretty closed off. Love told me it has something to do with his ex-girlfriend."

Avery wondered who this Lana was to Love and Drake, and made a mental note to ask Drake when she saw him again. El had mentioned Love was back in town and the two wanted to catch up over dinner. She'd ask then.

"Love didn't go into details about their business, but apparently she did a number on him when she left him," *Lana* continued. "I tried everything I could to get his attention, too, aside from parading naked in front of him. I even insinuated I'd be open to no-strings sex. He is a hottie."

"And he still didn't bite?" Hailey asked.

Avery held her breath, hoping that El hadn't bitten that heifer.

"No, not at all," Lana replied. "Anyway, she's back in town. You won't believe who she is."

"Who is she?"

"Avery Montgomery."

"Shut up. The creator of *The Preserves*?"

"Yep."

Avery wondered if that Lana woman knew she was in the exam room. But Drake had told her they'd kept her patient status under wraps, with only a handful of people knowing she'd been there. Granted, today, they'd pretty much opened the door by coming to the clinic during normal office hours. Avery had hoped they'd be able to get in and out without alerting the public or the paparazzi to her presence.

The voices moved farther away, and Avery let out a long breath. Under normal circumstances, she wouldn't care what any woman had to say about her relationship with El. No one knew what had happened between them but them. But in this case, the other woman's words bothered her.

Had she really left El in that state? Had he been so hurt by her that he'd closed himself off to other women as Lana had described?

Avery tapped a finger on the chair next to her and contemplated her next move. *Jess.* She needed to talk to her friend. Pushing the nurse call button, she waited.

"Can I help you, Ms. Montgomery?" the nurse asked as she walked into the room. "I just received a call that Dr. Laramie is running a little behind. Can I get you some water?"

Avery shook her head. "No, thank you. But I'm wondering if I can use a phone?"

The nurse smiled. "Sure."

The nurse pulled a cordless phone from the pocket of her scrubs. "Just dial nine first."

Avery took the offered phone and punched in a number. When Jess answered, Avery said, "Jess, I need you. I'm at the hospital, at my appointment. Can you come pick me up afterward?"

El stood at the door of his brother's office. He'd hated lying to Avery about where he was going, but when he read an email from Drake warning him that Lawrence was in town and roaming the hospital halls, he'd had to act.

Lawrence's executive assistant had already alerted his brother to El's arrival, so the visit wasn't going to be a surprise, like he'd hoped. But his older brother was going to hear what he had to say.

Cracking his knuckles, El formulated the words, planned the execution and prepared for various responses or excuses Lawrence could give. Finally, when he was ready, he knocked on the office door.

"Come in," his brother called.

El walked into the office. "Lawrence."

His brother looked up from a file on his desk. "El, what brings you by to see me?"

Growing up with Lawrence had essentially saved him from his uncaring parents, but it hadn't saved him from his selfish and domineering brother. Lawrence had always been more concerned with his money and his women and the Jackson name than about his children or El.

El suspected that was one reason each of them had gone into a different field of medicine—with the exception of Myles. El remembered clearly the day he'd announced to his brother that he was planning to practice psychiatry. The argument that followed had echoed in the house, drawing everyone from their respective spots to witness the carnage.

Lawrence had told him that psychiatry was beneath him, that El had consistently disappointed him after he'd sowed so much time and money into his education. It was pretty much the same conversation he'd had with Drake a few years later when Drake announced he would not be following in Lawrence's footsteps.

"Drake told me you were in town," El said.

"Not for long. I have to head to Los Angeles. Why?"

El scanned the office, noting the paintings on the walls and the shelf with ceramic pieces on it.

Lawrence had amassed an impressive portfolio of material things. He had a warped view of beauty, choosing to surround himself with priceless pieces of art, valued at hundreds of thousands of dollars.

"We need to talk," El said, cutting to the chase.

"Is this about the foundation your ex-girlfriend, Avery, is starting?"

El frowned. "How do you know about that?"

"Her friend Jess sent an invitation to the fund-raising gala to my office."

Surprised that Jess had moved so fast, El made a mental note to ask a few of his colleagues to attend and lend their support. "It's a very good cause, Lawrence."

His brother waved his hand in dismissal. "It's one of many. Not interested."

"Would you be interested if I were to take her back? Would you offer to donate to her foundation if she'd walk away from me, like you offered to pay off her college debt if she left me all those years ago?"

To his credit, Lawrence didn't flinch, didn't react at all. Instead, he steepled his hands together and leaned forward. His cold eyes met El's. "If that's what it took, yes. Listen, El, is there a point to this conversation? Isn't little Miss Montgomery ancient history?"

"Don't call her that."

Lawrence shrugged. "Okay. Isn't Avery long gone, doing her little drama on television?"

"That *little* drama has earned her status and is very successful. You should try being a little less judgmental. You know what? You've always acted like you're some pillar in the community because you donate to all the right causes and because your last name is Jackson. But you don't fool me. Your charitable endeavors are all for show because you don't really care about anyone else's plight. You only do things that benefit your bottom line."

"*Our* last name is Jackson. That means you have the same responsibilities I do. My grandfather and my father left a legacy that I will damn well preserve. If that means getting rid of people that threaten that legacy, I will."

"Why don't you like her?"

"I didn't say I didn't like her. But she's beneath you. She's not suitable for you."

What the hell could his brother tell him about preserving a legacy? Drake was only seven months older than the twins, and the product of one of Lawrence's many affairs.

El snickered. "That's rich coming from you. You've been married three times, *brother*. You have cheated on all of your wives, even going so far as to conceive a child with one of your mistresses. Was that behavior fitting for a Jackson? Was it Jackson behavior to treat your kids like ornaments you can bring out once or twice a year at hospital functions or for photo ops? I take that back. That is Jackson behavior because that's exactly how Mom and Dad treated me."

"Don't get crazy, El. You will respect me."

"Newsflash. I'm not one of your kids. I'm your brother. And respect is earned."

"Elwood."

"No, I'm sick of this. You harassed her, told her she wasn't worthy of me. Because of you, she left me."

"She left you because she followed the money, El."

"If she was following the money, she would have taken what you offered. That deal was sweeter, anyway, at the time."

"It didn't matter. As long as she did as she was told."

"Man, I swear, if you weren't old, I'd beat the crap out of you."

Lawrence frowned. "I'm not sure what's gotten into you, but none of this matters in the grand scheme of things. You and Avery are not together anymore."

"That's where you're wrong. Avery and I are working things out."

Sighing, Lawrence took a sip of his coffee. "Mark my words, El. If you let that woman back into your life, she'll hurt you."

It was just like Lawrence to not show remorse when confronted with the things he'd done. A few months ago, he'd conspired with Love's father, Dr. Leon Washington, to break Drake and Love up. He'd even gone so far as to pull strings to get Drake a Johns Hopkins fellowship to get him out of town. It had almost worked, too.

Fortunately for Drake and Love, it didn't. El wondered how Ian, Myles and Mel would fare with a father like Lawrence.

"El, what is it about Avery that has you losing your mind over her?" Lawrence snickered. "She's a beauty, but she doesn't have your pedigree. Her parents—"

"Are hardworking, devoted people who raised

their daughter to be the same way," El said, inter-
rupting his brother. "Avery is intelligent and determined and driven, and she has her own money. She
doesn't need mine. And guess what? If she asked, I'd
happily give her anything she wanted. But she hasn't
asked. She's never asked."

Lawrence leaned back in his chair. "Like I said,
nothing good will come of this. She may not have
taken *my* money, but she did leave for money."

"No, she left because you belittled and harassed her
and made her think she wasn't good enough for me."

Shrugging, Lawrence said, "She's not."

El swiped the papers from the desk and blared,
"Shut up. For once, shut up."

Lawrence simply stared at El as if he'd grown another head or turned blue. Sighing, he said, "What
would you have me do? I did offer to pay her off, but
that was years ago. As you've said, she has amassed
her own fortune and is living in another state. If you
choose to uproot your life, leave your career and family to go chase after a piece of ass, I can't very well
stop you. But please know this…when she leaves you
again or disappoints you again, don't bother coming
to me for anything."

"This is a joke, right?" El asked. "Since when do
I come to you for anything?" Slicing a hand in the
air, El said, "Forget it. I don't have time to argue with
you today, Lawrence."

"Like I said, El, you can do what you please."

"What I want is for you to respect her. Don't ever
say anything to her about our relationship. That topic

is not up for discussion. Matter of fact, how about you never speak to her again?"

Turning on his heels, El stalked out of the office, slamming the door behind him.

Chapter 15

El stormed through the halls back to the neurology clinic only to find Avery gone. He almost tore the hospital up looking for her, but his administrative assistant told him she'd dropped by to let him know that Jess was going to give her a ride home.

El wondered what had happened to make her call Jess, especially when he'd told her he'd be back. He dialed Jess's number, but didn't push the call button. Maybe it was just as well. Four days spent with Avery, filled with desire for her, had prevented him from looking at their situation logically.

The only thing on his mind was being with her. He was so enamored with her that he couldn't think straight. Before he knew it, he found himself in The Friends Meditation Garden at the hospital. The haven was created to restore, to provide comfort to patients, visitors and staff. He'd spent a lot of time there over the years when he needed a break or to center himself. Sitting on a bench, he let out a deep breath. He'd been angry with Lawrence before, but never so angry he wanted to literally wring his neck. If he hadn't been twenty years older, El would have been tempted to wipe the floor with his brother's salt-and-pepper mane.

"El?"

His head snapped up, and he was surprised to see Drake and Love standing before him, brown paper bags in their hands. Love was wearing blue scrubs while Drake wore green scrubs with a white coat. They both looked tired, but happy.

"Hey," he said. "Working a double shift?"

"Why do you ask?" Love asked, smoothing her hair back.

"He's trying to say we look rough, Love," Drake said. "In his El way."

El smiled, but he was sure it didn't reach his eyes. And Love would notice because she noticed things like that.

"You're not okay," she said, taking the seat next to him. "What's going on? I heard Avery was in town."

El looked up at Drake, who shrugged. "I couldn't keep the secret from my wife, El. Damn."

"Whatever, Drake," El said before addressing Love. "She is. But I don't want to talk about her. How are you? I'm glad you came back and saved me from Drake."

Love laughed. "Was he getting on your nerves?"

El smirked. "Every day."

"Eat all your food?" she asked.

"Hell, yeah."

"Hey," Drake said. "I'm standing right here."

"We know," El and Love said simultaneously.

Drake sat on the other side of El, effectively sandwiching him between the two of them. "We have news."

El glanced back and forth between Love and Drake. "You're pregnant?"

Love gave him a bright smile. "I am."

"That's amazing," El said, pulling them both into quick, yet strong, embraces. "I'm happy for you. When is the due date?"

"Christmas Eve," Love said. "Can you believe it?"

El couldn't believe it, but he was happy nonetheless. "Let's hope the baby comes before the holiday. Wouldn't want to shortchange him or her on gifts."

"I told Drake the same thing," Love agreed. "I want my baby to be able to celebrate *her* birthday in peace."

"*He* will be able to celebrate on Christmas Eve. It will just be an extra-special day."

El chuckled. "You two are made for each other."

Drake reached over El to hold Love's hand. "I can't imagine my life without her." And as if El wasn't sitting there, Drake leaned over and pulled Love into a kiss.

"Yeah, no. This is not happening." Standing up, breaking the two of them apart, El turned toward his family. "I'm here for you both. Whatever you need."

"Why you are avoiding talking about Avery?" Love asked. "What's going on with you?"

El shrugged, thinking of her and wondering what she was doing. "Just dealing with life. I found out something Lawrence did and confronted him."

"I would have paid to see that," Drake grumbled. "I just saw him with Myles a few minutes ago."

"Myles must have just met up with him, because I left Lawrence about a half an hour ago."

"What did Dr. Law do?" Love asked, taking a bite from her bagel.

El decided he needed to tell someone what happened. He started from the beginning, telling them how things had gotten so damn complicated.

"Wow," she said when he finished his story. "That's terrible. Poor Avery. That must have been hard."

"Damn, man," Drake said. "That's rough. No wonder she left. I'd want to be as far away from Dad as possible after that."

El really did understand why Avery had left him. It didn't change the fact that he'd been hurt by her actions, though. It just enabled him to be able to forgive her and move forward.

Yet there was a lingering thought in the back of his head they weren't done talking about the things that went wrong in their relationship. Professionally, he would advise a patient like him to seek counseling, or at least discuss everything before he made a decision to continue a relationship that may be best extinguished.

Of course, he hadn't taken his own advice when he'd slept with her, not just once but multiple times. He couldn't see past the ache in his body when she was near him.

"How did Dad react when you confronted him?" Drake asked.

"As you would expect, like he did nothing wrong. Or he didn't care. Both reactions pretty much suck."

Love sighed. "I wish Avery would have talked to you about it before she left. But I understand why she didn't."

El also wished Avery had told him earlier what Lawrence had said to her. That was the part that really bugged him. It felt like she hadn't trusted him to be able to make up his own mind about her. She hadn't trusted him to protect her against Lawrence.

"Yeah, but think about it," Drake said. "Put yourself in her shoes. She didn't grow up around money. You said yourself, she was sheltered and doted on by Phil and Jan. I can understand why she let him get to her the way she did. There may have been a part of her that had always been insecure about the differences between you, and Dad's words amplified it."

Sometimes Drake could be downright profound. "That's what I think, too," El said.

"So what are you going to do?" Drake asked.

El shrugged. "Hell if I know. She was supposed to wait for me at the clinic today, but when I got there she'd already left with Jess. I'm not sure what to think."

"Why waste time thinking about it?" Love suggested. "Just go talk to her and hear her reasons from her. Love you, El, but I always thought you should have done more when she left."

The truth was brittle. Love was right. He could have pushed her to give him a reason. If he'd done that, instead of retreating within himself, they might be already married with a kid by now.

* * *

"What are you going to do?" Jess asked Avery.

Avery and Jess were seated on Avery's parents' porch on the hanging swing.

El hadn't called or texted. Avery couldn't help but wonder if he would. It had been an hour since she'd left the hospital. She'd left a message with his assistant, letting him know where she'd be. Yet he hadn't called to check on her.

When she'd arrived back at her parents' house that afternoon, they were elated that she was back and that she'd regained her vision. Avery was touched by the emotion her father had shown, because he was normally stoic and unemotional. But the way he'd broken down when she told him she could see him would stay with her forever. He wouldn't stop hugging her and telling her he loved her. There hadn't been a dry eye in the house and Avery couldn't say she'd have had it any other way.

"You have to make some important decisions, Avery," Jess said. "You can't go on like this where El is concerned."

Shrugging, Avery said, "That's why I called you. I don't know what to do. Every part of me is telling me I should fight for him. I've already told him I would fight for us. But after I overheard that conversation, I'm not sure I am the woman he needs in his life."

"Why do you think that?"

"Because I hurt him. I'm the one who broke his heart." Avery recalled their big argument when El had told her she'd "gutted him" when she left.

"You're also the one that's healing his heart, Avery. You can't just give up because of something you heard, not even from him. Don't you think you owe it to him to have a conversation with him?"

Avery knew Jess was right, but she couldn't shake the feeling that *she* was right, too. "You don't understand."

"I do understand. You're scared, and I understand fear. I deal with it every day, every single time I think I'm ready to date again. You're going to have to get over it. If you want to be happy, you're going to have to find a way to move past your mistakes, Avery. For the first time in months, you look rested. Healthy. As your friend, I'm ecstatic, and I know that has something to do with El. So I'm on his team. I want you two to make it work."

Jess made sense. Avery had pushed for them to have the hard conversation, and now she was letting his words coupled with the words of two strangers cloud her judgment.

"What if it can't work? While we were away I told him I wanted him to forgive me. I told him I'd work for it. After that, we were so caught up in the passion of it all that I didn't realize that he'd never actually told me he forgave me, Jess."

"So? He's with you. Doesn't that mean he forgives you?"

Avery wanted to believe that Jess was right, but the doubt had already crept in, and she needed to hear the words from him. "I don't know. The only thing I know for sure is that he wants me. And I can feel that he loves me. That doesn't mean he trusts me. It doesn't mean that he's forgiven me for hurting him."

Jess squeezed her hand. "El would have never been

with you again if he didn't trust you. He's not even that type of person and you know it."

"It was so perfect up there, Jess. We were in our own little world, just me and him." Avery didn't want to believe it had been a waste of time. In fact, she knew it hadn't. But now, in the light of day and away from the paradise they'd created, the complications and conversations they'd chosen not to deal with were rearing their ugly heads.

"It can be that way here, too," Jess told her.

Avery looked at her best friend, her sister. She looked tired, worried. "Jess, have you been resting?"

"How can I rest when I'm worried about you?"

"Listen, I thank you for taking care of me when I needed you. I appreciate that you've stepped in for Luke and acted as my assistant." While they were gone, Jess had secured a date and venue for the fund-raising gala next month, of her own volition and without prompting from Avery. She'd even hired an event planner who'd sent out special invitations to several key members of the community. "But...you're fired."

Jess's eyes widened. "What? Why?"

"Because being my assistant is not your job. You already have one of those. You're my best friend, and it means the world to me that you've helped me, but you have your own life. I can't have you keeling over from the stress of mine."

"We help each other," Jess said. "I want to be here for you, just like you're there for me when I need you."

"Fine. You can be here for me as my best friend. And I want you to head my foundation."

Jess blinked, her hand rising to her mouth. "Avery, really?"

"Yes. You're the perfect person for the job. I know you love what you do for the university, but I'm willing to pay you a top salary if you'd work with me on this." Avery hadn't ironed out all the details, but she trusted Jess and knew her friend would put her all into the foundation because she was as vested in the mission as Avery was.

"Wow, I don't know what to say."

"Say yes," Avery prompted.

"Yes! I'll do it."

Avery hugged her friend, taking comfort in Jess's embrace.

Jess pulled back and grinned. "You do realize I've never been fired from a job before."

Shrugging, Avery said, "Well, technically, I wasn't paying you so it doesn't really count."

Jess barked out a laugh and handed Avery her planner. "Fine. You can have this back."

Opening her book, Avery scribbled a note in the margin. "We'll talk more about the gala tomorrow morning and you can tell me all about this venue you booked."

They fell back into a comfortable silence as they rocked in the swing. When Avery noticed El's car pull into the driveway, she sucked in a deep breath. "He's here."

El walked up to the porch. "Hi," he said, shoving his hands into his pants pockets.

"Hey." Jess stood. "I'm going to leave so you two can talk."

When she was gone, El joined Avery on the swing. "You left."

Swallowing, Avery nodded. "I had to think."

"About?"

"Us. I overheard somebody named Lana talking about you, and it got me to thinking."

El frowned. "Lana? Where did you see her?"

"She was standing outside my exam room, chatting away with someone named Hailey about you. And me. I mean, I couldn't write this stuff if I tried."

"What did she say?"

"Who is she?"

El leaned back and folded his arms over his chest. "Love's cousin. Love and Drake tried to hook me up with her a few times. She's a nice person, but I wasn't feeling her in that way. So it never went anywhere."

"Well, that's pretty much what she said. She also mentioned that Love had told her how I'd left you in a bad way."

El nodded. "Well, that's true. I already told you that."

"I know. But I need to know if you're truly ready to move forward, if you forgive me. Because if you don't, then there's no sense in continuing this, whatever it is between us."

"Avie, we've already established that you hurt me. I know I've probably hurt you. Those things don't just go away overnight. My intention is to move forward with you. But it's going to take time. So much has happened. We have to take this one step at a time."

"That's fair. I hope you understand why it's so important to me to know that you forgive me."

"I do. But at the same time, you need to understand that forgiveness is an action. It has layers to it."

Avery nodded solemnly. "I get it. I just… I don't know. I kind of feel like we have to get everything out in the open to move forward."

"Avery, you still have a lot of healing you need to do."

"But I feel fine. The only thing I'm uncertain about is…"

"Me?"

She shook her head. "No, I'm sure of you. I'm sure that I love you. I'm sure that you love me. But loving someone and being able to truly put the past behind are two very different things. I don't blame you if you can't, but I need to know."

El tilted his head, eyeing Avery. "I will admit there is some apprehension on my part. We've been through a lot, Avie. But I'm clear on what I want. I want to try. I'm committed to trying with you."

Avery swallowed. "Okay."

"There's still so much we have to discuss," he continued. "You still live in Atlanta. And I live here. We have to figure out what that means for us."

"With the foundation being based here, I'll be here more often."

"But you have a job that requires you to live in another state, Avie. I don't expect you to give that up, because it's a part of you. What I do expect you to do is to keep the lines of communication open. We can spend some time discussing the particulars." He wrapped his arm around her and placed a kiss on her forehead. "I saw Lawrence today."

Avery tensed in his arms. "Really?"

"He mentioned receiving an invitation to the fund-raiser."

"Oh," Avery said. "So he was one of the community members who received a hand-delivered invitation?" When he frowned down at her she explained, "Yeah, Jess is phenomenal. She's already reserved a venue, and hired an event planner. They sent out a few invites. I offered her a job today."

"Wow. Jess has been a busy woman."

"She has, and I'm excited to work with her on this." Avery kicked up her feet. "What did he say about the invitation?"

"Don't count on him attending."

Avery lowered her feet, setting them firmly on the cement porch. "I'm glad he's not coming. I don't want anyone there that will cause confusion or ruin the evening."

It hadn't even been twenty-four hours since they'd returned to Ann Arbor, and there was already tension between them. Avery didn't like it one bit. "Will you be my date?" she asked, meeting his gaze.

El smiled. "I will. On one condition."

Groaning, Avery asked, "You and your conditions. What is it?"

"Come home with me tonight."

Avery peered over at him, let her gaze wander over his profile. He was so strong, so male, so sexy, so El. "Honestly, I'd strongly consider following you to Duck World if such a thing existed. Everything I have, all the awards, all the fame, all the money… None of that matters without you."

El chuckled before standing. Glancing down at

her, he held out his hand. "Then let's go. I promise I won't take you to Duck World, or even to Disney World where the ducks roam free to attack."

Avery laughed, then slid her hand into his and let him take her to his home.

Chapter 16

Avery's breath caught in her throat when she peered through the peephole and saw Thomas Brown on the other side. *Oh, my God.*

It had been a few days since they'd returned to Ann Arbor, and Avery had kept true to her word to El and her doctors, and not worked on the show. Instead, she'd focused on the foundation and the upcoming gala, finalizing the details.

Ann Arbor was the perfect choice for her foundation headquarters. It was her hometown. She loved the area and she'd been inspired by her neighborhood and her college life to create the hit show. She'd already started looking at commercial property as well as residential. If she was going to spend more time in Michigan, she needed to purchase a home there eventually.

She and El had discussed a possible move for her, and had even thrown around the idea of him spending time with her in Atlanta.

Sucking in a deep breath, she opened the door. "Thomas?" she said. "What brings you here?"

Thomas was her boss and one of the network executives who'd bought the television rights to her novel. Unlike other executives, he'd seen something in her that made him select her to pen the series pilot instead of a screenwriter. She'd forever be grateful.

It was rare when the actual author of a book optioned for film or television was given the chance to write the screenplay or script.

Thomas was a tall, brown-skinned man who'd had a meteoric rise to prominence at the network that owned *The Preserves*. She considered him one of her mentors in the business and would often ask herself "What would Thomas do?" when dealing with people.

"I wanted to check on you. Jess is very accommodating, open with the updates, but I wanted to see for myself how you were doing."

Avery motioned for him to come in. She'd spent the night at her parents', instead of with El, and they'd run out on a few errands. Thomas stepped into the house and she led him to the kitchen. "Coffee?" she asked.

"No, thank you." Thomas eyed her. "What's going on, Avery? You've dropped off the grid, and you know that's not a good idea in this business. One day too many out of the game could be a detriment for your career."

"I know, Thomas." Avery grabbed a bottle out of the refrigerator. "Water?" When he shook his head, she opened it and guzzled a large portion. "Walter told me he's been communicating with you, and I'm sorry I didn't give you call personally after my health scare. Doctors told me to stay put and unplug while I healed."

It was the patented answer she'd given to anyone who asked. But she knew Thomas wasn't buying it when he said, "Avery, I asked you what happened. I don't want the press version. I need the truth."

Sighing, Avery sat down on the stool. Deciding to be honest and let the chips fall where they may, Avery told Thomas almost everything about the stroke. She left out the part about losing her sight.

"And there is no residual damage?" he asked, concern in his brown eyes. Thomas acted like he could be an old friend of her father's, as if he'd known their family for many years, even though he'd only known them for a few. He'd met her parents and Jess, and had all their numbers. Over the past few weeks, he'd contacted all of them to get hold of her, but she'd purposefully avoided talking to him. He was older, mid-sixties, but he was young at heart. He ran five miles every morning and ate healthily. It was why he was in such good shape.

Avery shook her head. "No," she lied. Although her sight was back, she didn't know if there was any residual damage because she still had a depth perception problem. Her ophthalmologist had also suggested she start wearing eyeglasses. Her appointment with the optometrist was tomorrow.

"When will you be able to come back to work?"

Avery tapped her chin as if in deep thought. "Um, I'm not sure. Initially, the doctors told me six weeks."

Thomas blinked. "Let me tell you what's going on. Maybe that will help you make your decision."

Dread filled Avery's gut at the tone in Thomas's voice. "Just tell me."

"The network loved your new show idea. They want to buy it, they want you to write it, they want to give you creative control over casting. Oh, and they approved the new script you sent over for *The Preserves*."

Surprised, Avery stuttered, "W-what? Really?"

"Yes. But there is a catch."

Deflated, Avery waited for him to finish, wondering what she would have to do to make it happen.

"They want you present in Atlanta first thing tomorrow morning."

"Tomorrow? Thomas, I can't leave right now." Avery immediately thought of El. They'd made even more progress over the last few days, and she'd felt secure in the knowledge that they were on the right track. "I haven't been cleared for travel."

"Avery, listen to me. If you want your job, you need to be there. Now, I may be able to stall them for a few days, but that's it. They want you to report to work as soon as possible."

Sighing, Avery nodded. "Please see what you can do about stalling them. I need to clear any travel plans with my doctors." *And El.*

Thomas nodded, and they continued to talk about *The Preserves*, the new show and everything that would be expected of her over the next several months. Avery had wanted this for so long. She'd wanted the respect of the network, the respect of her peers. She wanted people to see that Avery Montgomery tag in the opening credits and know they were about to be treated to a well-written television show.

When Thomas left an hour later, headed straight for the airport, Avery sighed and plopped down on the couch. As much as she wanted this, and despite the fact that she'd assured Thomas she'd be present, she wasn't sure it was worth losing what she'd worked hard to rebuild with El.

So now she had to figure out how to make this work, keep her job at the network, and run her foundation.

El arrived at Avery's parents' home after work that day. He'd decided not to stay late again. For three days in a row he'd left work on time, even when he'd been tempted to stay and spend more time in the emergency room. It was the Avery effect. He'd been pleasantly surprised when she'd continued to push off work per the doctor's orders. And he'd been determined to meet her halfway by cutting back on his own work schedule.

The time spent watching movies and eating popcorn, playing Monopoly, taking walks through the neighborhood was priceless. The nights they'd spent together had only cemented his love for her.

When he entered the house, he called out to her.

"Up here," she said from her bedroom. She'd texted him earlier to say that her parents were out and that she had the house all to herself. El had smiled when she suggested they take a trip down memory lane—him sneaking upstairs and making love to her in her childhood bedroom.

Now in her doorway, he paused when he noticed

her sitting on her bed, her laptop in her lap, typing furiously.

She looked up at him with the reading glasses he'd purchased for her a few days ago perched on her nose. She smiled. "Hey."

Frowning, he stepped into the room. "Hey." Leaning down, he kissed her brow before sitting next to her on the bed. "What are you doing?"

"Working," Avery confessed. "My boss came to see me today."

El didn't need her to finish to know what was coming next. The network had called and she would go running. "And?"

Avery rubbed her face. "I have to go back to work."

"In Atlanta?"

She nodded. "They approved my scripts and my new show idea. But they've requested that I return as soon as possible."

"What about your doctors? You haven't been cleared to leave yet."

Averting her gaze, Avery said, "I have. After Thomas left, I called Dr. Laramie. He told me that I could fly to Atlanta, but that I would need to return for my follow-up appointments at least once per month for the next six months. He also told me he could refer me to a specialist down in Atlanta if I preferred."

"Ah," he said.

"El, I tried to stall him. I told him I couldn't leave. But it was pretty much leave or lose my job. And I can't lose my job."

"Is your job worth your life?"

El knew he was probably being a bit unreasonable. Well, a lot. Many people had strokes and were able to resume normal activities after several weeks. But he knew Avery. Once she went back to work, she'd push herself. Again. And maybe next time she wouldn't be so lucky. Maybe next time she'd be dead.

"Don't say that, El."

El blinked away those thoughts. "What am I supposed to say?"

She shrugged. "I don't know. That you understand?"

"I don't understand."

"How could you not? You work hard every day. You put in extra hours. You love your job. Why can't you understand that I feel the same way about mine?"

"Because I didn't almost die! Because I didn't leave *you* to accomplish my goals in life. But it's cool. You go ahead and leave. It's probably for the best. At least I won't have to watch you work yourself into an early grave." He was so consumed with his conflicting emotions that his words came out harsher than he intended. "I'm sorry. I didn't mean to snap."

Avery shot him a look of disbelief. "Come on, El. You expect me to believe that you didn't mean it? Usually, when someone is angry, they speak the truth."

But El really hadn't meant it. His first instinct was to hurt her because she'd hurt him. It was classic transference, and he was upset with himself for going there with her. "No, I really didn't mean it. I'm just upset."

"No, you haven't forgiven me."

Her observation smacked him over the head and

he bolted to his feet. "Really, Avery? I haven't for-given you?"

"No. You haven't." She stood. "I think you tried hard, but I don't think you ever did." She walked over and peered up at him. "I get that you're scared, but me going back to work doesn't mean that I'm leaving you."

El closed his eyes. He was scared. Scared to lose her.

"Avery, you're not superwoman. How do you pro-pose to handle everything? Something is going to slip through the cracks." *Would it be him*?

"That something is not you, El."

"I don't know if I can trust that, Avie."

Avery reeled back and he knew his words had hit her hard. But he had to be honest. There were no ifs, ands or buts. Life without Avery wouldn't work for him. At the same time, he couldn't bear to see her work herself into another stroke trying to make ev-erything work. He knew she would try, but he didn't think it was possible to write two shows, run a foun-dation and work on a relationship with him. He'd rather let her go than have her try to choose him and lose herself.

"El, I won't tell you that it doesn't hurt to know that you don't trust me, because it does. I do under-stand your position, though. The only thing I have is my word right now, because this is still new, un-charted territory for both of us." She stepped forward, and he closed his eyes, letting her warmth sooth him.

"It's not just you being here with me, Avie. I can't watch you work yourself…" He swallowed. "I lost you once. I almost lost you again. I can't do it again. I wouldn't survive it."

"You won't lose me. I don't want to go back to that time before we reconnected." Avery squeezed his hand. "The pain without you in my life was unbearable, which worked for my creativity. But my heart…without you is a shell. If you can truly forgive me, I can't promise you that I won't work too hard or be so engrossed in my work that I forget to eat or forget to relax. But I can promise I'll love you and I'll never hurt you again. I'll be the woman you deserve. I want you. I love you, El."

Chapter 17

Two weeks later, Avery entered the ballroom of the hotel where the Avery Montgomery Foundation fund-raising gala was in full swing. She was dressed to the nines in a floor-length cobalt-blue gown. Thomas had arranged for her to borrow a stunning sapphire and diamond necklace from an Atlanta jeweler for the event, which accentuated her outfit. Her hair was styled in a bob with a long bang. Reporters flanked the room to get a view of the people in attendance, and she'd stopped to pose more than a few times before she'd entered the massive space.

As she greeted guests, she marveled at how the event planner had transformed the traditional room. Jess had done a phenomenal job with the event. The ballroom was lovely already with its high ceilings and breathtaking crystal chandeliers. But the decor, in cobalt blue, silver and black, made it even more beautiful.

According to Jess, they'd raised over two hundred thousand dollars so far, and she expected more to come in. The ballroom was full of doctors, university faculty, local celebrities and a few national celebrities, as well. And the cast of *The Preserves* had flown in to support her, which had been a pleasant surprise. All in all, she considered the event a success.

She scanned the room, hoping El would be there. But she hadn't seen him. She did see Drake and Love. They'd both greeted her with warm hugs and wide smiles. When she'd asked about El, Drake had simply shaken his head. Her huge overture two weeks ago hadn't gone over the way she'd hoped. Instead of agreeing to work together, he'd left her that night.

Soon after, she'd caught a flight back to Atlanta to begin work again. Her doctors had cleared her for normal activity but scheduled her for three-month checkups over the next year. There were no residual effects from her vision loss, and Avery was grateful.

Walter had successfully renegotiated her contract with the network, building in time to work on her foundation and other interests. There was even a clause that allowed her to work from Ann Arbor when necessary. Once she was satisfied with the terms, she threw herself into her job, immediately communicating with staff that she would not be available each day after she left the office. It was her form of self-care. It didn't mean she wasn't working after hours. But it did mean that she wouldn't be so available for her job that she couldn't enjoy her life. Not that she'd enjoyed anything since leaving Michigan. In fact, she was pretty miserable.

When it came time to fly back, she'd been giddy with excitement to return to Ann Arbor, which was a major shift. She'd even put an offer on a plot of land and was in the process of hiring a builder to construct her new home. Her parents had decided to stay in Ann Arbor, so she was especially happy to see them when she'd arrived earlier that morning.

"Are you ready to give your speech?" Jess asked from behind her.

Turning to her friend, she said, "Yes. No. I'm nervous."

Jess had given notice at her job, and true to form, had been an awesome addition to her team. Avery couldn't have done it without her.

"Why?" her friend asked. "You got this, Avery. You worked hard."

Avery smiled at her best friend. Jess was radiant in a floor-length navy blue gown. Her hair was swept up in a loose bun. She was stunning.

"No, you've worked hard," Avery said. "I can't thank you enough for loving me, for supporting me."

Jess embraced her tightly. "I'm always going to support you, just as you've always supported me. We're sisters in every sense of the word."

"I wish El was here," Avery admitted.

Jess brushed a strand of hair from Avery's face. "I know. Maybe he'll come around."

Avery hoped so. Life without him sucked. Plain and simple. She wanted him with her. No, she needed him with her.

"Listen." Jess squeezed her shoulders. "Don't

worry about El right now. Concentrate on what a huge success this event is. Think about how many young women you're helping afford college just by attaching your name to the cause. Think about what you want to say in your speech that will inspire others to do similar acts within the community."

Avery shot Jess a wobbly smile, fanning her face to keep the tears from falling. "You always make me want to cry."

"Girl, you do not cry. You're Avery freakin' Montgomery."

Laughing, Avery pulled Jess into another tight hug.

Later, Avery was standing against the wall going over her speech notes when she looked up to find Dr. Law approaching her.

Avery sucked in a deep breath as he neared her, ready for battle. When he was finally standing in front of her, she said, "Dr. Law."

"Avery Montgomery." Her name on his lips sounded clipped, curt.

"What can I do for you?"

Dr. Law sighed. "I have to say, I'm impressed. Your foundation is the talk of the town."

Holding her head high, Avery said, "Thank you. But you should know, I didn't do this for your approval."

"I guess I deserve that."

"My parents worked hard to give me a good life. No, they didn't travel in your circles. They couldn't write a check for my tuition. But they loved me, they supported me. I'm the woman I am because of them, and because of El. I let your words get into my soul back then, but I'm not that girl anymore. So if you came here to threaten me or belittle me in any way, I suggest you keep it moving."

The man sighed before taking a sip of the drink in his hand. "And I deserve that, too. Avery, it takes guts to do what you've done with your life. I respect that. I'm sorry."

And without another word, he nodded and walked away. Avery wasn't sure how to feel about what had just transpired, but she didn't have time to think about it.

Thomas introduced Avery as the speaker seconds later, and her father escorted her to the front of the room. As she stood, scanning the faces of those who came to support her, she felt a sense of pride. They were there because they wanted to give back to little girls, young people of color who might not have the resources to go to college. They were there because they believed these young women were worth their investment. They believed in her.

Avery started her speech with a tribute to her parents for their unwavering support, to Jess, to a few others who had been an important part of her life and to El. Embracing her fears, she'd chosen to admit them to the audience, including her duck story, which drew a few giggles from the crowd. In her conclusion, she talked about her stroke, which elicited shocked gasps and whispers. But she brought it home and spoke about the desire to give back, to leave a legacy.

"And I—" Avery looked up from the podium and her eyes widened at the sight of El standing in the back of the room. Her gaze dropped for a second, so she could regain her composure, and when she looked back up he was gone.

Taking a deep breath, she smiled at her mother who was standing with tears in her eyes in front her. She scanned the expectant faces of her guests, swallowed and continued. "I want to thank you for supporting me, but more importantly, for supporting our future. Thank you."

Okay, so that's not how she'd planned on ending her speech. But the sooner she could get down from the stage, the sooner she could find El. As she left the podium she was greeted by several people, but all she wanted to do was tell them to give her a minute. But that would be rude, and she couldn't be rude to people who were donating to her foundation.

Jess was at her side a moment later. "You did an amazing job, Avery. I'm so proud of you. But that wasn't the end to your speech."

"El," Avery said simply.

Her friend's head whirled around as if looking for him. "He's here?"

"I saw him in the back of the room during my speech."

Avery hurried through the crowd, peering up at random men's faces. No El. Finally, after about twenty minutes of looking, she figured he'd left and decided to try to enjoy the rest of her evening.

Closing her eyes, she took several deep breaths. *No, Avery, you can't cry. This is not the time to look like a raccoon. You'll ruin a perfectly good smoky eye.*

"There's no crying at events where people are giving you money."

Avery froze and her eyes popped open. "El," she

breathed. "Are you really here? Or are you a figment of my imagination?"

"I'm here." He stepped closer, traced his thumb under her right eye. "Remember what I said. No crying, Avie."

"You just made that up," she said with a nervous laugh.

"I'm pretty sure you'd scare most of the donors if you wound up with dark, wet eyes."

"Well, maybe you should put me out of my misery?"

El gazed into Avery's topaz eyes. She was a vision in cobalt blue. He'd been unable to keep his eyes off her since he'd arrived a half hour ago. Drake and Love had egged him on, urging him to reveal himself to her, but he'd hung back. He wanted to wait until she was done with her speech. Well, that's what he'd told himself. Really, he just wanted a chance to look at her, gaze at her soft skin and expressive eyes. He wanted to listen to her articulate why the Avery Montgomery Foundation was so important to her. He'd been silently cheering her on during her speech, surprised when she'd revealed so much about her personal journey. He was proud.

The last couple of weeks without her had been torture for him. And according to Drake and Love, it had been preventable torture. Avery had been right. Her going back to work wasn't the same as her leaving him. Work was work. But they were El and Avery. She was *his* Avery, and he couldn't let her live another day without letting her know that.

"I'm sorry," he mouthed.

"You're sorry?"

He nodded. "I guess I was more scared than I wanted to admit. But not just of you moving away. I'd almost lost you, and I was terrified that you would slip right back into your old habits and, perhaps, have another stroke. I was worried, and I handled it the wrong way."

"But, I—"

"Wait. I need to say this. I want you to know that I forgive you. I know you need to hear the words, and I never said them."

"El," she whispered. "You're going to make me cry and you said crying wasn't allowed."

He chuckled. "I did say that, didn't I?" Leaning his forehead against hers. She smelled of daisies and a hint of champagne.

Avery searched his eyes. "I've been calling you."

El had received Avery's messages. Although he knew it was wrong to ignore her, he couldn't bring himself to answer. He'd needed to center himself, gain some control over his emotions before he talked to her. "I'm sorry I didn't pick up."

"I forgive you."

Unable to resist her mouth, El touched his lips to hers in a soft kiss, drawing a moan from her throat.

"I love you, El," she said when he pulled away. "I negotiated my contract to allow me to spend more time here. I bought land, and I'm building a house. We can make it work. I can fly here on the weekends during shooting. And when we're not shooting, I'll be here working on the foundation. I promised myself that if you let me love you again, if you opened your heart to me again, that I wouldn't take it for granted.

I don't want to waste any more time. My life only works with you in it. So please—"

El interrupted Avery's words with a searing kiss, claiming her with such an intensity he surprised himself. The heat of her body against his, the scent of her, made him want to carry her out of there and worship her all night.

She tasted like warmth and comfort, like everything he'd ever need for the rest of his life. She was as essential to him as air, and he would do anything to keep her with him.

When he pulled back, Avery mouthed, "Wow."

The smile that bloomed across her face then was like a lit match against his skin, setting his body on fire. "Wow is right," he agreed, nuzzling his nose against her cheek.

"I take it you believe me."

He chuckled. "I do."

"So you'll stay with me?"

"I'm not going anywhere. I promise." He placed a lingering kiss against her lips again, before nipping her bottom lip gently. "Avie?" When she opened her beautiful eyes and smiled at him, he grinned. "I love you, too."

Epilogue

Avery stood at the entrance to the park, her fingers nestled in the crook of her father's arm.

He patted her hand tenderly. "Ready?"

Through wet lashes, she nodded. "I'm ready."

The music started, and Phil Montgomery led Avery down the aisle. As Avery approached *her* El, she couldn't help the wide grin that formed across her lips. She was finally marrying the love of her life. As she scanned the few guests, she couldn't believe the day had finally come.

El had proposed the night of the gala, presenting her with a beautiful princess-cut solitaire. And Avery had lost her composure, crying so hard, everyone stopped what they were doing to watch the show. But she hadn't hesitated and shouted "Yes" before jumping into El's arms.

Of course, after the proposal, Jess had whisked her away to the bathroom to fix those raccoon eyes. But Avery hadn't cared how she looked because she had everything she wanted in that moment.

Unfortunately, the public cared, and a picture of her sobbing and looking a hot mess ended up on Instagram in a matter of seconds. She'd been the subject of quite a few blog posts and tweets.

The headlines had been a source of entertainment for El. She recalled his laughter when one blog had suggested that El and Avery had a secret child. Then, there was the one that implied that Blair Wallace was planning to interrupt the wedding and steal her away.

As she neared El, she noted the tears standing in his eyes and her heart soared. They'd chosen to marry at the Sleeping Bear Dunes. It sounded simple, but it was anything but. There were permits to be pulled, security to hire, tents to set up, money to spend. In short, Jess was a raving lunatic because she'd decided to plan the wedding.

Yet as Avery looked at her best friend, standing to her left, bawling her eyes out, it was hard to believe just a few hours earlier she'd been cursing out everyone within earshot.

Drake stood to El's right as his best man.

They'd decided on a short, traditional ceremony— no personalized vows, no long drawn out songs. Just pledges to love each other in sickness and health, for richer or poorer. But Avery had drawn the line at "obey." Instead, she said that she would obey his request to not sing in the shower or burn dinner because she was too busy to remember to turn the oven off. At that last part, El had tilted his head toward the sun and laughed.

They were pronounced husband and wife in front of fifty of their closest friends and family members. Then El had lifted her up in her Vera Wang gown and carried her down the aisle to the waiting limo.

Inside the limo, on their way to the same Italian restaurant where she'd begged him to forgive her and admitted her undying love for him again, he'd asked the driver to take the scenic route and made love to her right on the floor of the limo.

Now, as they pulled up to the intimate reception, he pulled her into his side and kissed her brow. "Avery Jackson."

"Avery Montgomery-Jackson," she corrected.

El squeezed her tight, and she giggled. "Avery Jackson," he repeated. "I love you more today than I did yesterday. I'll love you more tomorrow than I did today."

She smiled at his use of her own words. "You could've made up your own declaration of love, you know."

The rumble of laughter in his chest made Avery feel like the luckiest woman in the world.

"How about this? The end."

"I like the sound of that. I love you, Dr. Elwood Jackson."

"And I love you, Mrs. Avery Jackson."

* * * * *

KIMANI™ ROMANCE

COMING NEXT MONTH
Available June 19, 2018

#577 UNDENIABLE ATTRACTION
Burkes of Sheridan Falls • by Kayla Perrin

When a family wedding reunites Melissa Conwell with Aaron Burke, she's determined to prove she's over the gorgeous soccer star who broke her heart years before. Newly single Aaron wants another chance with Melissa and engineers a full-throttle seduction. Will Melissa risk heartbreak again for an elusive happily-ever-after?

#578 FRENCH QUARTER KISSES
Love in the Big Easy • by Zuri Day

Pierre LeBlanc is a triple threat: celebrated chef, food-network star and owner of the Big Easy's hottest restaurant. Journalist Rosalyn Arnaud sees only a spoiled playboy not worthy of front-page news. Their attraction tells another story. But when she uncovers his secret, their love affair could end in shattering betrayal…

#579 GUARDING HIS HEART
Scoring for Love • by Synithia Williams

Basketball star Kevin Koucky plans to end his career by posing naked in a magazine feature. When photographer Jasmine Hook agrees to take the assignment, she never expects a sensual slam dunk. But he comes with emotional baggage. Little does she know that Kevin always plays to win…

#580 A TASTE OF PLEASURE
Deliciously Dechamps • by Chloe Blake

Italy is the perfect place for new beginnings—that's what chef Danica Nilsson hopes. But one look at Antonio Dante Lorenzetti and her plan to keep romance out of her kitchen goes up in flames. The millionaire restaurateur wants stability. Not unbridled passion. Is she who he's been waiting for?

Get 2 Free Books,
Plus 2 Free Gifts—
just for trying the Reader Service!

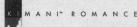

YES! Please send me 2 FREE Harlequin® Kimani™ Romance novels and my 2 FREE gifts (gifts are worth about $10 retail). After receiving them, if I don't wish to receive any more books, I can return the shipping statement marked "cancel." If I don't cancel, I will receive 4 brand-new novels every month and be billed just $5.69 per book in the U.S. or $6.24 per book in Canada. That's a savings of at least 12% off the cover price. It's quite a bargain! Shipping and handling is just 50¢ per book in the U.S. and 75¢ per book in Canada*. I understand that accepting the 2 free books and gifts places me under no obligation to buy anything. I can always return a shipment and cancel at any time. The free books and gifts are mine to keep no matter what I decide.

168/368 XDN GMWW

Name _____ (PLEASE PRINT)

Address _____ Apt. #

City _____ State/Prov. _____ Zip/Postal Code

Signature (if under 18, a parent or guardian must sign)

Mail to the **Reader Service:**
IN U.S.A.: P.O. Box 1341, Buffalo, NY 14240-8531
IN CANADA: P.O. Box 603, Fort Erie, Ontario L2A 5X3

Want to try two free books from another line?
Call 1-800-873-8635 or visit www.ReaderService.com.

*Terms and prices subject to change without notice. Prices do not include applicable taxes. Sales tax applicable in NY. Canadian residents will be charged applicable taxes. Offer not valid in Quebec. This offer is limited to one order per household. Books received may not be as shown. Not valid for current subscribers to Harlequin® Kimani™ Romance books. All orders subject to approval. Credit or debit balances in a customer's account(s) may be offset by any other outstanding balance owed by or to the customer. Please allow 4 to 6 weeks for delivery. Offer available while quantities last.

Your Privacy—The Reader Service is committed to protecting your privacy. Our Privacy Policy is available online at www.ReaderService.com or upon request from the Reader Service.

We make a portion of our mailing list available to reputable third parties that offer products we believe may interest you. If you prefer that we not exchange your name with third parties, or if you wish to clarify or modify your communication preferences, please visit us at www.ReaderService.com/consumerschoice or write to us at Reader Service Preference Service, P.O. Box 9062, Buffalo, NY 14240-9062. Include your complete name and address.

SPECIAL EXCERPT FROM

*When a family wedding reunites Melissa Conwell
with Aaron Burke, she's determined to prove she's over the
gorgeous soccer star who broke her heart years before.
Newly single Aaron wants another chance with Melissa
and engineers a plan for a full-throttle seduction. Will
Melissa risk heartbreak again for the elusive dream of a
happily-ever-after?*

*Read on for a sneak peek at
UNDENIABLE ATTRACTION,
the first exciting installment in author Kayla Perrin's
BURKES OF SHERIDAN FALLS series!*

"This is certainly going to be one interesting weekend," she muttered.

"It sure is."

A jolt hit Melissa's body with the force of a soccer ball slamming into
her chest. That voice… A tingling sensation spread across her shoulder
blades. It was a voice she hadn't heard in a long time. Deeper than she
remembered, but it most definitely belonged to *him*.

Holding her breath, she turned. And there he was. Aaron Burke.
Looking down at her with a smile on his face and a teasing glint in his
eyes.

"I thought that was you," he said, his smile deepening.

Melissa stood there looking up at him from wide eyes, unsure what
to say. Why was he grinning at her as though he was happy to see her?

"It's good to see you, Melissa."

Aaron spread his arms wide, an invitation. But Melissa stood still, as
if paralyzed. With a little chuckle, Aaron stepped forward and wrapped
his arms around her.

Melissa's heart pounded wildly. Why was he doing this? Hugging her as if they were old friends? As if he hadn't taken her virginity and then broken her heart.

"So we're paired off for the wedding," Aaron said as he broke the hug.

"So we are," Melissa said tersely. She was surprised that she'd found her voice. Her entire body was taut, her head light. She was mad at herself for having any reaction to this man.

"You're right. It's going to be a very interesting weekend indeed," Aaron said, echoing her earlier comment.

He looked good. More than good. He looked…delectable. Six feet two inches of pure Adonis, his body honed to perfection. Wide shoulders, brawny arms fully visible in his short-sleeved dress shirt and a muscular chest. His strong upper body tapered to a narrow waist. A wave of heat flowed through Melissa's veins, and she swallowed at the uncomfortable sensation. She quickly averted her eyes from his body and took a sip of champagne, trying to ignore the warmth pulsing inside.

Good grief, what was wrong with her? She should be immune to Aaron's good looks. And yet she couldn't deny the visceral response that had shot through her body at seeing him again.

It was simply the reaction of a female toward a man who was amazingly gorgeous. She wasn't dead, after all. She could find him physically attractive even if she despised him.

Although *despised* was too strong a word. He didn't matter to her enough for her to despise him.

Still, she couldn't help giving him another surreptitious once-over. He had filled out—everywhere. His arms were bigger, his shoulders wider, his legs more muscular. His lips were full and surrounded by a thin goatee—and good Lord, did they ever look kissable…

*Don't miss UNDENIABLE ATTRACTION
by Kayla Perrin, available July 2018
wherever Harlequin® Kimani Romance™
books and ebooks are sold.*

Want to give in to temptation with
steamy tales of irresistible desire?

Check out **Harlequin® Presents®**, **Harlequin® Desire** and **Harlequin® Kimani™ Romance** books!

New books available every month!

ROMANTIC suspense

*Armstrong Black doesn't do partners, and Danielle Winstead
is not a team player. To find the criminal they're after, they
have to trust each other. But their powerful attraction throws
an unexpected curveball in their investigation!*

*Read on for a sneak preview of
SEDUCED BY THE BADGE,
the first book in Deborah Fletcher Mello's
new miniseries,
TO SEDUCE AND SERVE.*

"Why did you leave your service revolver on my bathroom
counter?" Armstrong asked as they stood at the bus stop, waiting
for her return ride.

"I can't risk keeping it strapped on me and I was afraid one of
the girls might go through my bag and find it. I knew it was safe
with you."

"I don't like you not having your gun."

"I'll be fine. I have a black belt in karate and jujitsu. I know how
to take care of myself!"

Armstrong nodded. "So you keep telling me. It doesn't mean
I'm not going to worry about you, though."

Danni rocked back and forth on her heels. Deep down she was
grateful that a man did care. For longer than she wanted to admit,
there hadn't been a man who did.

Armstrong interrupted her thoughts. "There's a protective detail
already in front of the coffee shop and another that will follow you
and your bus. There will be someone on you at all times. If you get
into any trouble, you know what to do."

Danni nodded. "I'll contact you as soon as it's feasible. And
please, if there is any change in Alissa's condition, find a way to

let me know."

"I will. I promise."

Danni's attention shifted to the bus that had turned the corner and was making its way toward them. A wave of sadness suddenly rippled through her stomach.

"You good?" Armstrong asked, sensing the change in her mood.

She nodded, biting back the rise of emotion. "I'll be fine," she answered.

As the bus pulled up to the stop, he drew her hand into his and pulled it to his mouth, kissing the backs of her fingers.

Danni gave him one last smile as she fell into line with the others boarding the bus. She tossed a look over her shoulder as he stood staring after her. The woman in front of her was pushing an infant in a stroller. A boy about eight years old and a little girl about five clung to each side of the carriage. The little girl looked back at Danni and smiled before hiding her face in her mother's skirt. The line stopped, an elderly woman closer to the front struggling with a multitude of bags to get inside.

She suddenly spun around, the man behind her eyeing her warily. "Excuse me," she said as she pushed past him and stepped aside. She called after Armstrong as she hurried back to where he stood.

"What's wrong?" he said as she came to a stop in front of him

"Nothing," Danni said as she pressed both palms against his broad chest. "Nothing at all." She lifted herself up on her toes as her gaze locked with his. Her hands slid up his chest to the sides of his face. She gently cupped her palms against his cheeks and then she pressed her lips to his.

Don't miss
SEDUCED BY THE BADGE by Deborah Fletcher Mello,
available June 2018 wherever
Harlequin® Romantic Suspense books and ebooks are sold.

www.Harlequin.com

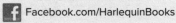